MURDER AT THE MAISON DE BALZAC

An Inspector Henri Corbet Mystery

Elizabeth Cowley Tyler

MINERVA PRESS
ATLANTA LONDON SYDNEY

MURDER AT THE MAISON DE BALZAC:
An Inspector Henri Corbet Mystery

ISBN 0 75410 623 3

First Published 1999 by
MINERVA PRESS
315–317 Regent Street
London W1R 7YB

Printed in Great Britain for Minerva Press

MURDER AT THE MAISON DE BALZAC

An Inspector Henri Corbet Mystery

To Honoré de Balzac,
that giant of French literature,
who was a spokesman for his time
and whose Paris continues to inspire
and electrify the modern reader.

About the Author

Elizabeth Cowley Tyler is the author of a series of mystery novels featuring Inspector Henri Corbet of the Paris Police. *The Madeleine Murders* is the first novel in the series, and *Murder at the Maison de Balzac* is the second.

Ms Cowley Tyler lives in Cambridge, Massachusetts, and is currently employed as an Official Court Reporter for the Superior Court of the Commonwealth of Massachusetts. She holds a Bachelor of Arts in English Literature from Elmira College and a Master of Arts in French Language and Literature from Middlebury College. She has lived in Paris and has travelled extensively in France, England, Germany and Russia.

Acknowledgements

I am indebted to Isabelle Naginski, Robert Frye, M. Eustace Erwin and Eleanor Ellis for reading the manuscript and making many helpful suggestions. In particular, I thank Isabelle Naginski for her course at Harvard on the Nineteenth-Century French Novel in which we read Balzac in light of the core concept of the invisible crime.

Kay Nelson, Nicola Phillips, Rona Troderman-King, and my cat, Mimi, have continued their love and support, and I thank them.

The staff of The Hotel St Louis, my *hôtel particulier* in Paris, have provided me with comfortable lodging and encouragement during my research visits.

Inspector Henri Corbet and I are also indebted to Patricia Wells for her wonderful books, *Bistro Cooking* and *The Food Lover's Guide to Paris*, to Pierre Franey for his *Cooking in France* and to Linda Dannenberg for her *Paris Bistro Cooking*.

Mais je vous vois entrant dans le monde littéraire et journaliste avec des illusions. Vous croyez aux amis. Nous sommes tous amis ou ennemis selon les circonstances…

But I see you entering the world of literature and journalism with illusions. You believe in friends. We are all friends or enemies according to the circumstances…

Illusions perdues
Honoré de Balzac

Les sentiments nobles, poussés à l'absolu, produisent des resultats semblables à ceux des plus grands vices.

Noble sentiments carried to an extreme can produce the same results as the greatest vices.

Les jouissances de la haine satisfaite sont les plus ardentes, les plus fortes au coeur.

The strongest joys of the heart are those of vengeance.

La Cousine Bette
Honoré de Balzac

But Paris is an ocean. Throw in the plummet, you will never reach bottom. Survey it; describe it. However conscientious your survey and careful your chart, however numerous and concerned to learn the truth the explorers of this sea may be, there will always be a virgin realm, an unknown cavern, flowers, pearls, monsters, things undreamed of, overlooked by the literary divers. The Maison Vauquer is one of those strange monstrosities.

Père Goriot
Honoré de Balzac

Chapter One

Inspector Henri Corbet quickly climbed the stairs leading out of the Passy Métro stop. He pulled his coat tightly around his bulky middle and snuggled his neck down into his scarf. The early January wind whipped his collar-length gold and silver hair about and assaulted his solid frame. He detested hats and gladly risked losing body heat through his head in cold weather.

As he reached the corner of the rue Raynouard, he entered a telephone booth to call Gilet at the Quai des Orfèvres. Stealing time from the Préfecture now made him uncomfortable, particularly with his promotion to Chief Inspector on the line. His discomfort was tempered, however, by the sense of freedom he felt at being out of the line of conflict. Gilet would keep an eye on things while he was gone, and the warm kitchen at the Maison de Balzac would feel good.

Corbet headed for 47 rue Raynouard. He enjoyed the story of how Balzac had lived there for several years in hiding from his creditors under the name of Monsieur de Breugnol. The house had a secret door for a quick exit should one of them call. Balzac's taste for luxury and his tendency towards over indulgence endeared him to Corbet who wasn't very adept at handling his own money or controlling his appetite.

Food was on the agenda today. He had promised Marie that he would help cook the buffet dinner for the annual meeting of the Society of the Friends of Honoré de Balzac.

Her friend, Monique de La Tour, was being honoured for her new book, *Balzac and the Creative Process*.

A cream of mussel soup and a ragôut of lamb with white beans were among suggestions Corbet had made. They were readily accepted by the soirée committee on the condition that the Inspector would cook the main dish. He had agreed but had insisted that he must prepare the braised lamb at least one day in advance of when it was to be eaten so that its full flavour could develop. So, he had left the Préfecture on this Friday morning for a couple of hours to oblige a friend and to indulge his hobby.

He descended the steep stairs leading to the front of the house which was set down two levels from the street. He entered the curved pentagon-shaped entryway, rang the bell and waited what seemed like a long time before being admitted by Michel, a doorman who had been at the Maison de Balzac for many years. The odour of alcohol that surrounded him like a cloud was not lost on Corbet. He had noticed it on prior visits. Michel was not a live-in employee as were Henriette and Jacques who came up the stairs from the kitchen to greet him.

Corbet exchanged kisses with Henriette and shook Jacques's hand, and they went down the narrow stairs into the kitchen in a single file with Henriette going first, Corbet second and Jacques bringing up the rear, dragging his lame leg after him.

'A little early for you to be away from the Préfecture, hey, Corbet? On your off hours again, are you?' Jacques knew how to hit a nerve.

'Just stepped out for a little bit. Gilet knows where I can be reached, if necessary.' Corbet hoped his firm tone would keep Jacques at a comfortable distance.

The warmth from the oven of the grand, black, multi-burner stove wrapped itself around him like a blanket. The wine, sea and herb smell of the fish fumet that Henriette had just made filled the room.

Corbet had come to know Henriette and Jacques from his visits to the Maison de Balzac. He found it relaxing to read in the library and avail himself of the considerable collection of books and material by and on Balzac. The library was located on the lowest level, and the large red-tiled kitchen was right beside it. Often as he sat at his table reading, his nose would be treated to wonderful smells coming from Henriette's kitchen. He was unable to resist introducing himself to her and trading cooking secrets. Their friendship had grown so that each time he visited, if it were around lunch time, he could count on being served one of her marvellous meals.

While Corbet liked Jacques well enough or didn't really dislike him, there was no great affinity between them. Jacques seemed rather pedestrian, and Corbet found Henriette's sensibility much more to his liking. This was not lost on Jacques, and Corbet often sensed his silent resentment. Today's needling was a more direct expression of that hostility. So when Jacques excused himself immediately to go to the garden tool shed, it did not surprise him.

Upon entering the kitchen, Inspector Corbet headed straight for the large black stove, picked up the lid on Henriette's fumet, and took a long whiff.

'This is going to taste just heavenly, I know.' His large-featured face glowed. He smiled broadly at Henriette.

'Oh, Henri, you are such a good audience for me.' She beamed her appreciation. 'I've ordered everything you told me to, and the butcher has cubed the meat in equal parts from both the shoulder and the leg of the lamb just as you instructed. The beans are soaking in the pantry.' She reported duties completed like a soldier to her general.

Corbet grabbed a large, white apron from one of the hooks, tied it around his girth, rubbed his hands together and approached the great wooden table in the middle of the room to survey the bounty which Henriette was assembling for his approval. There was a mountain of lamb, fresh tomatoes, carrots, onions, bunches of fresh thyme and parsley, bay leaves and whole cloves.

'Ah, these,' he said holding up the fresh thyme and pointing to the whole cloves, 'are the secret to the flavour.' Henriette smiled at him and nodded her head.

As he surveyed the ingredients for his creation, Corbet stood for a moment like a conductor before a symphony orchestra, arms poised in mid air. He bent to lift two huge black cast iron pots from the cupboards below to the great gas burners. He covered the bottom of each pot with equal portions of butter and olive oil. He then browned the large quantity of lamb in batches, taking care to remove each finished portion to a warm platter to wait for the final cooking while he browned the others.

He could feel himself start to relax as the meat began to sputter and sizzle in the pan. His anxiety over absenting himself from the Préfecture for a while and over the fact that he had gotten off to a bad start with the new Commissioner of Police diminished.

He had been truly grieved when Commissioner Mamon had retired. Not only did he miss the pleasure of working with him, but he also knew that getting the promotion he sought to Chief Inspector would not be easy with a new Commissioner, and particularly this one. After the de La Roche case, Corbet had become a rather hot item at the Quai des Orfèvres. It was his bad luck now to seek a promotion from somebody with whom there was a natural antipathy, bad chemistry. Also, the rivalry between him and his colleague, Renard, was intensified by the fact that they now both sought the same promotion.

Then there was Marie, whom he cherished. They had become very good friends. She seemed to like and need his company. She was still healing from her loss, and Corbet hesitated to press his suit on that ground. He also feared being told what he sensed, that he was a dear and good friend but nothing more. He wanted to be able to hope.

While he browned the meat, Henriette busied herself with chopping the tomatoes, onions and carrots. As she bent over the chopping board, a lock of her black, curly hair fell over her face. She stopped, rinsed her hands and pulled it back. She was an attractive, full-figured brunette with firm skin who could have been anywhere from forty to fifty. Corbet suspected that she was older than she looked.

With the meat all browned, it was now time to divide it up into the two large black pots and assemble the rest of the dish. Corbet sprinkled the lamb in each pot with flour, mixed it well, and let it cook for a few minutes. He then added white wine and water and deglazed the pans, making sure to scrape up all of the brown bits from the bottom. With the addition of the tomatoes, onions, carrots, herbs and spices, he brought the mixture to a simmer to be covered and cooked for about an hour and fifteen minutes.

'And now to the beans,' he beamed at Henriette who had just finished thoroughly washing the large, wooden table. 'We'll do them today, too. They can keep in the refrigerator overnight and just be reheated tomorrow.'

Henriette agreed and went into the pantry to get them. When she didn't come back in a few minutes, Corbet went to the door to see what was holding her up. He found her searching the pantry cupboards in a somewhat distressed state muttering that she had left the beans on the counter the night before. He began to help her search.

'Looking for these?' Jacques appeared at the door of the pantry with the pot of beans in his hands. 'I was bringing them to the kitchen earlier when I remembered something I had left in the tool shed. I just put them down in the hallway for a bit. No harm done.' Henriette sighed in annoyed relief, took the beans from him and handed them to Corbet.

Jacques left saying that there was something he needed to tend to upstairs.

Once back in the kitchen, Corbet drained the beans of their soaking liquid while Henriette got out two more large cast iron kettles. Each was filled with the beans, cold water, bay leaves, cloves and thyme and brought to the boil to be cooked for about forty-five minutes.

As the beans and lamb began to cook and give off their inviting fragrance, Corbet sat down and gladly took the bread, pâté and Sauternes Henriette offered him. He had just bitten into the lovely pâté de foie gras with truffles when he heard Jacques dragging his leg in the hall outside of the kitchen. He pushed himself through the door and glared at Henriette who looked rather helplessly at Corbet. Jacques was cursing and muttering under his breath. Michel had been found slumped over the desk in Balzac's writing room. Some visitors to the museum had reported it to the guard in the ticket booth. He was dead drunk and had to be taken home.

'Seems to me he ought to have been let go a long time ago,' Jacques muttered half under his breath. 'Must know someone in high places to get away with what he does.' He grabbed a chair and angrily joined Corbet and Henriette at the table.

The more the room began to fill with the wonderful odour of the cooking lamb and beans, the more sour Jacques's expression became.

Chapter Two

With a full stomach and a mild glow from the evening's wine, Corbet nestled further down in his large, mahogany sleigh bed and pulled the goose-down duvet around his bulk like a bear preparing to hibernate. His movement stirred the sleeping Michelet who looked up at him, yawned, readjusted his position and purred himself back into a slumber.

He glanced at the gold box on his night table wondering whether his resistance to Henriette's tarte Tatin at the soirée should be rewarded with the last two Madame de Sévigné chocolates nestled in the corner of the box. He decided to go for it, seized the first one and bit into it.

With the dark soft sweetness of the chocolate spreading through his mouth, he returned to his book. He was coming to the final scene in Balzac's *Père Goriot* where Goriot's daughters send their empty carriages to attend the funeral of their all-too-generous father. He remembered that the first time he had read that passage he had dropped the book on his chest, closed his eyes and felt a profound sadness and horror at the depiction of such cold-hearted selfishness. A shudder ran down his spine as he turned the last page.

He let the book fall gently on his chest. What a contrast the sad tale was to the joy he had seen at the soirée that evening. He saw the radiantly beautiful face of Monique de La Tour who seemed to relish the honour paid her by her colleagues. Marie had been more ravishing than usual. He could feel himself becoming more and more drawn to her.

The sense of promise of good things to come softened his reaction to Balzac's tale.

The large black phone on the bedside table gave off its loud, buzzing ring. He moved the book and picked it up.

'Just now?' He inquired of the voice at the other end. 'You mean this evening? A few minutes ago? But I was just there.' Inspector Corbet glanced at the clock. It was 2 a.m. He had left the Maison de Balzac about midnight at the conclusion of the festivities and now Gilet was on the phone reporting that they had just found a dead body. His last view of the now-dead woman flashed before him. He tried to ignore the feeling that he was being pursued by some evil force.

'She was found in Balzac's writing room near his desk? You've secured the scene, of course?' Gilet assured him that he and Leroux had done their jobs. The body would be sent to Ménager as soon as Corbet authorised it.

'I'll be right there.' He gingerly pushed the bed covers aside, gently placed his copy of *Père Goriot* on the bedside table, grabbed the lonely remaining chocolate and popped it in his mouth. Michelet, now in a deep sleep, remained in the bed and didn't seem to notice his departure.

Chapter Three

The cab sped through the empty streets of Paris from the rue de Buci to the rue Raynouard. A steady rain had begun to fall, and it was difficult to see out of the windows. Corbet was still shifting gears into investigative mode, wondering how this could have happened, asking himself if he had noticed anything unusual about the behaviour of the victim or anyone else at the soirée. The short answer was no, yet he must have missed something. He felt somehow he had failed to do his job, even though his job usually didn't begin until after the fact. Never before had he been present at a crime scene such a short time before a murder was committed.

He thought the soirée had gone very well. Certainly his main course had received rave reviews from everyone. He reached in his pocket and felt a group of small pieces of paper. He had come away with a number of requests for the evening's recipes, and this made him uncomfortable, because he didn't believe in sharing his cooking secrets with the public at large. First of all, he really didn't cook from what most people knew as recipes. He cooked from something like instinct and preferred to trade culinary secrets with those of similar talent. However, he had taken the names of the people at the soirée because he simply couldn't say he'd rather not. He would deal with the consequences of that later.

He got out of the cab in front of the Maison de Balzac, paid the driver, descended the stairs to the main entrance and rang the bell. This would make three times he had entered this building in the past forty-eight hours, each with a different goal and result.

'Oh, Henri, I'm so glad you're here.' Henriette opened the door. Her face was streaked with tears, and her hands shook slightly as she closed the door behind herself and Corbet. He couldn't help noticing what a contrast this woman was to the woman he had left earlier that evening, a woman flushed with the pleasure of a job well done and glowing with the compliments she had received on her soup and tarte Tatin. Corbet wished for a moment he could turn the clock back to that time of comfort and joy if only for Henriette's sake.

'Inspector, it's in here.' Gilet's lanky form appeared in the hallway, and his long arm pointed in the direction of Balzac's writing room. Corbet felt himself deliberately slow his pace to prepare himself for the shock of what he was about to encounter. Crime scenes were not his favourite part of an investigation. He didn't like seeing people dead. He swallowed hard and entered the room.

The first thing he saw was a shattered porcelain cafetière which lay in smithereens on the floor. It was the antique container once used by Balzac in his all-night coffee and work marathons.

Using that fractured object as a point of focus, Corbet let his eyes be guided just to the left of it where he saw strings of unkempt blonde hair wet with some kind of dark liquid that didn't look like blood. The head to which the hair was attached was twisted to one side and tilted slightly upward. Corbet stared into the expressionless, marble-like eyes of Véronique Lefèvre. Every time he looked into the eyes of a corpse, he hoped that this time he would see them move in some sort of response, some proof that this had been a false alarm. The cold agates didn't move.

His eyes followed down the body dressed in a black evening dress with a black, cashmere shawl twisted around it. She looked very frail and helpless. He returned to the eyes and thought he saw some plea for help struggling under the cold stare. He shook his head and looked again. This time what stared back at him was dark and lifeless.

He reached down to check the pulse in her carotid artery. The body was slightly cool but not at all stiff. Finding no pulse, he glanced beyond the sprawling figure to the left side and saw more smashed porcelain. This time it was a tea or coffee cup, one of the Limoges set that had been used at the soirée for the dinner party.

Inspector Corbet also noticed that in the clenched fist of her right hand she appeared to be clutching a sheet of paper. He paused a moment considering whether he would try to pry the fist open. A shudder ran down his back as he reached gingerly for the clenched hand. With a little force he was able to open it and release the paper. On it was written in a fine hand a rather lengthy quotation from a Balzac novel, *Le Lys dans la vallée*. He read it to himself.

> *How weak and powerless is human justice. It only punishes open acts. Why does death and shame come to the murderer who kills with a blow...? Why does a happy life and esteem come to the murderer who drips poison drop by drop into the soul and eats away at the body to destroy it? How many murders go unpunished? What joy for elegant evil! What acquittal for homicides caused by moral persecution!*

Inspector Corbet fell back on his heels, his head fairly reeling at the power of the sentiment in the quotation. He gingerly put the note in his pocket. Gilet and Leroux were standing by anxiously. They knew Corbet well enough not to speak too quickly when he arrived at a crime scene.

When Inspector Corbet finally stood up, his line of vision went right to the large marble bust of Balzac by David d'Anger which he had always admired when visiting the writing room. The large well-formed head, the long nose with nostrils slightly flared, the strong cheekbones, embedded in ample flesh, the long hair reaching to the nape of the neck were an impressive interpretation of Balzac's enormous strength. Corbet's glance shifted to Balzac's mahogany desk and chair. They seemed unharmed. The chair was drawn slightly away from the desk as though someone had sat in it, had gotten up, and had forgotten to push it back.

As his eye scanned the room, he noticed another piece of paper in the corner on the far side of the podium which held the bust of Balzac. He bent to pick it up. In the same hand it was another quotation, this time from *Père Goriot*. Corbet smoothed out the paper and read it to himself.

> *If it were possible to become the heir of a man whom no one had ever seen or heard of who lived in the depths of China by pressing a button to kill him, who among us would not press that button and kill the Mandarin?*

Corbet took a deep breath. The very quotation from *Père Goriot* which had inspired Dostoyevsky's *Crime and Punishment*. Putting the paper in his pocket, he became aware of the din and clatter made by the crime scene group milling out in the hall and in another of the display rooms of the museum. He knew that they were anxious to get to work. Of course, all of the evidence would have to be preserved. Corbet took a little more time to look around. He could find no blood, no weapons anywhere. It could have been death from natural causes. Ménager would have to determine that. Probably wishful thinking.

With a sigh and a shrug of his great shoulders, he issued the order. 'Roll the cameras.' The photography team came in and began to shoot the crime scene from all angles. Corbet went out in the hallway. At the far end he saw Henriette white-faced and hugging herself. He shot her a glance of compassion and hoped she understood that he could not talk with her just now. He would soon have to interview her formally.

The front door opened and a large, lumbering man with bright red hair and sleepy blue eyes entered the foyer. It was Ménager. Corbet felt reassured by his appearance. They had worked together for some time now. He was about the best forensic pathologist in Paris, but you would not hear him boast about it. He did his job and let the work speak for itself.

'Henri, we meet again.' Ménager extended his long arm to reach for Corbet's hand.

'Jean-Pierre, it's always a pleasure,' Corbet said with a little wink of irony at his long-time colleague.

'At least that,' was all Ménager replied.

He followed Corbet down to Balzac's writing room where the photographers were just winding up, and the hard evidence men were getting ready to comb the scene and gather their treasures. They all scattered when they saw the tall redhead enter the room.

'That's all right, I just want a quick look at the body before you begin your collecting.' Ménager swung a long arm across his body and to the right, a courtly gesture to establish his territory. He bent his long frame over the motionless Véronique Lefèvre. He, too, felt her carotid artery and peered closely into her glazed eyes. Casting a quick glance at the area surrounding her body his eye focused on a piece of the broken Limoges cup that had a large red lipstick mark on it.

'We'll need to compare that with what's on her lips,' he said gesturing towards the chip of cup. 'Of course, I won't know for sure until I get her open, but it could be cardiac arrest from poison. I'll need to know what she was drinking.' He looked up at Corbet. 'When your men are through here, let me know. I'll send my men over to bring her to the Quai de la Rapée. I'm going back there now to wait for you.' He stood to his full height, leaned back and stretched his back a bit putting his hands on his haunches. 'It gets harder as you get older.' Corbet nodded in agreement.

'All right, men, go ahead and finish your collection.' Corbet felt suddenly tired and considered waiting until morning to question Henriette. The image of her distress flashed across his mind, and he reconsidered. Maybe the questioning would help her come to terms with this dreadful experience. Besides, Jouvet would be watching everything he did now more closely than ever. It was bad enough that he had been a guest at the party where the crime had taken place. He had to do it now. He went out into the hall and headed to where Henriette was standing.

'Let's go down to the kitchen. We need to talk.' He took her arm and led her towards the narrow stairs leading down to the kitchen. 'Where's Jacques?' He suddenly realised that it was curious that he wasn't around.

'Oh, he was here at first but said he felt he would just be in the way. He's gone back to bed.' Corbet gave a little shudder as he reached the bottom step. That man was unbelievable. His wife had just discovered a dead body in what for all intents and purposes was their home, and he had gone to bed. He shook his head and entered the kitchen which was still warm from the night's activities.

A quick look around told him that, as usual, Henriette had been efficient. The large, wooden table looked calm and clean, showing no evidence at all of the evening's frenetic use. All of the china had been washed and put away. The large, black multi-burner stove looked lonely and neglected. Only the faint lingering scent of the ragôut of lamb gave any hint that the kitchen had been recently used. Corbet found himself flaring his nostrils, trying to grasp the odour to let it take him back to a happier time in this kitchen.

'Would you like some tisane or coffee or something stronger?' Henriette seemed to regain some composure when on her own territory.

'Actually, if you have a little Armagnac, it might go down well.' Corbet didn't normally drink in the middle of the night, but these were rather extraordinary circumstances.

'I also have some tarte Tatin left if you would like some.' She headed for the pantry door.

'That would be wonderful.' After all he had not really eaten his due portion at the soirée. Serving him his Armagnac and tarte seemed to further calm Henriette. He took his first forkful. With the sweet tartness of the apples fortified by cinnamon and butter melting in his mouth, he knew he could begin to do what he had to do. He savoured his forkful of tarte, swallowed it and chased it with a swig of Armagnac.

'Thank you so much. You always know just what and when to feed me.' He smiled up at Henriette who now looked strong enough to undergo the interview.

'Now, tell me just what happened this evening.' Henriette sat across from Corbet at the wooden table in the corner of the kitchen. She folded her hands one on top of the other and took a deep breath.

'I had just finished up down here. You know, Henri, it really took me so long tonight to clean up. Longer than usual. I had begun to do it even before the main course was served upstairs. I didn't finish until just before...' She trailed off and looked at Corbet whose warm brown eyes expressed his compassion for her distress.

'Go on, Henriette,' was all he said.

'Well, you see, I went upstairs one last time to check for any stray dishes or food left about up there. I had checked all of the rooms but the writing room. I almost didn't even bother to go in there, but then I thought better of it. Elise, the maid they hired to assist me this evening, had already gone home. She had been in charge of gathering up used dishes and cups and disposing of food.

'At any rate, I headed for the writing room with thoughts of Jacques's experience with Michel the day before spinning in my head. Michel hadn't been around during the day, but I knew that he would be back. I was so distracted by my thoughts that I almost missed seeing her. She was dressed in black, and it was dark in there. When I saw the dark bulk on the floor, I turned on the light, and there she was staring up at me. I'll never forget that cold gaze. My heart nearly stopped.' She paused, drew a deep breath and took a sip of the tisane she had made for herself.

'Was anyone else around when you went upstairs?'

'No. It was all very quiet. I didn't see anyone. Jacques had gone to bed early. He usually does. In fact, I had to wake him up to tell him what had happened. He wasn't very happy about it, either.' Corbet shook his head.

'Go on, Henriette.' She looked determined to finish.

'I was shocked to see the body of someone I had just seen at a party. Somehow that made the whole thing more eerie. I remember when I saw her earlier that evening noticing how drawn and depressed she looked. With her gaunt cheeks, lifeless eyes, damaged, yellowish skin and the broken blood vessels in her nose, she looked ill – but there was no way I would ever have imagined that she would turn up dead at the end of the evening.'

'I'm sure I feel the same way, Henriette. I, too, noticed how out of sorts the woman looked. I'm sure the only people who expected this outcome were the ones who may have been involved in making it happen, whoever they are, and that's what we must find out. What else did you notice?' Corbet pressed on.

'Well, after I got over the shock of seeing her lying there, I did notice the broken cup and cafetière. All I could think of was how upset the Society of the Friends of Honoré de Balzac would be about the fact that the cafetière was broken. It's a real antique. Balzac actually drank coffee made in that. The Limoges cup I knew would also upset them. The set is very old, too, but not as precious as the cafetière.'

'I see.' Corbet wondered how upset the Society of the Friends of Honoré de Balzac would be about the fact that Véronique Lefèvre was dead. Indeed, he wondered how upset her sister, Monique, would be. 'Then what did you do?'

'Well, first I went to wake up Jacques. It took him a little while to understand what I was telling him. At first, he didn't believe me. He thought I was pulling a joke on him. He wouldn't get up. Then I really started to cry, and he got up and came upstairs to see what I had seen. I told him I was going to call the police right away. He said maybe we should wait until tomorrow morning. I said I didn't think we should. He then accused me of just looking for an excuse to get in contact with you in the middle of the night.' Her eyes pleaded with him to understand.

'Of course you did call, and you did the right thing.' He finished his last forkful of tarte and took his last swig of Armagnac.

'Yes, I did. I got your assistant, Officer Gilet, who said he would contact you and come right down. I'm glad you're here, Henri. Somehow it helps.' She smiled softly at him.

'Yes, well, now, during the evening while the soirée was in progress, can you remember noticing anything or anyone unusual?'

'Not really. Let me think. I was so busy running up and down serving and cleaning up, I really can't say that I did notice anything out of the ordinary. As I told you, I did notice Véronique Lefèvre. She was so drawn looking, and she looked as though she were looking for a place to hide. I guess I couldn't help noticing the contrast between her appearance and demeanour and that of her sister, Monique. Of course, the evening was to honour Monique, but nevertheless, it still seemed strange. I think that's about it.' She got up, took the glasses and dishes to the sink and began cleaning them.

Corbet, too, had noticed a contrast between the two sisters during the soirée. In fact, it was the first time he had met either one of them. He had been particularly taken with the subtle beauty of Monique, and he had found himself sneaking furtive glances at her all evening. Marie had told him so much about her that he felt he knew her in some way. His only acquaintance with Véronique was through her work in *Le Monde*. Since his favourite kind of reading was not acerbic criticism, he was not one of her more avid fans.

'Oh, I almost forgot. The other thing that I noticed that seemed a bit odd was that Madame Ballard, I think her name is, kept pestering Jacques to let her leave early by the back door that Balzac had used to avoid his creditors. She said she had always wanted to exit the house that way. I think he finally did let her use it. She left the party around ten or so. I don't think she returned.' Henriette closed the cupboard door after putting away the dishes, and once again, the kitchen was completely tidy.

'Did you hear her speak to Jacques or is this something he told you about after the fact?' Corbet leaned back in his chair.

'Well, now that you mention it, I don't think I actually saw her talking to him. It was really from his complaining that I got the information. He always complains whenever anyone asks anything of him. He doesn't like to do favours unless he can see clearly that there's something at the other end of it for him.' Her voice gradually trailed off with the last words.

'He won't be convicted for his largesse, that's for sure,' Corbet couldn't help but add. 'In any case,' he continued, 'he told you he let her out the back door around ten o'clock?'

'Yes, that's right.' Henriette folded her hands and continued to look softly at Inspector Corbet.

'You never saw this Madame Ballard after that?' he asked again to make sure.

'No, I never saw her again the whole evening. In fact, I saw her very early in the evening and never saw her after that. You must remember that I was very distracted with my work and all. That's what I remember.' She shifted her position in her chair and looked as though she wanted the interview to be over.

Corbet considered the situation for a moment. 'That's it for now. I may have to talk to you more later on, though.' He thought he had better warn her.

'But of course, Henri, any time later. I'm very tired now.'

'Of course you are. Thank you, Henriette. *À bientôt.*' He got up and climbed the steep stairs to see how the men were coming with the collection of evidence.

Chapter Four

As he mounted the stairs of the building at the Quai de la Rapée, Corbet felt that the Paris Police morgue and forensic laboratory were the eeriest places on earth during these early morning hours. He entered the long hallway and went to the end of it where a light shone through a glass door with large bold letters, LABORATOIRE. He opened the door, and he was hit by the smell of alcohol, formaldehyde and other odours he could not identify. At the end of the room there was a tall figure in a white coat bent over a long steel cart like a ghost performing some primeval ritual. At the sound of footsteps, the large white figure straightened up revealing a thick mane of red hair. Ménager was at work. The body had arrived, and he was losing no time.

'Ah, Corbet,' he said turning his head slightly to the side. 'Welcome. I'll keep on working if you don't mind. You can watch if you like. I know how much you like this part of the job.' He gave Corbet a warm wink and continued to rummage with his white-gloved hands in the visceral area of the corpse of Véronique Lefèvre. 'Have your boys begun to work on that cup yet?'

'All of the evidence has gone to the lab. I'm sure they're at it now. I told them to begin with that piece of Limoges,' Corbet reassured him.

'Good. I was right. It was cardiac arrest, but I think she had some help. Her liver is pretty far gone. If she hadn't died of whatever killed her now, it wouldn't have been long before her system rebelled against the overload of poisons she was putting into it. I've taken a number of blood samples, and they're at the lab. I suspect she was a very heavy drinker and that she was using barbiturates, but I don't think that's what actually killed her. It might have helped in combination with other things. We'll see.' He flashed a large-toothed grin at Corbet who looked up at his considerable height.

'You don't think it was something in the food at the soirée?' He thought it best to get that out of the way immediately.

'I'm not sure. I don't think it's poison in food, but I won't know for certain until we get the lab tests back on stomach contents. That would put you on pretty shaky ground, hey, Henri?' Corbet was surprised that Ménager could joke about a thing like that. He didn't quite know how to respond.

'Come on, Henri, I'm only teasing. I know it couldn't have come from your food. But everyone in Paris is going to be watching this one. She was pretty well-known, you know.' Ménager continued his rummage in the cavity as though looking for buried treasure.

'Yes, I know. I'm certain that Jouvet won't miss this opportunity to make my job more difficult, to say nothing of the interference I'm going to get from Renard. I don't look forward to this one. Jean-Pierre, I'm really going to need all the help I can get from those in my camp.'

He moved around to the other side of the steel cart in an attempt to lock eyes with Ménager who obliged him with a reassuring glance and continued his search. Corbet stood by for a moment just staring blankly at what under other circumstances would have made him sick to his stomach. It was as though he didn't really see what Ménager was doing. However, when Ménager reached further down into the cavity and pulled out the heart, Corbet started, backed away and went around to the other side of the table where his view of the dead body was obstructed by Ménager. He felt his stomach give a lurch and hoped that he could keep down the tarte and Armagnac to say nothing of the evening's meal. He had never actually been sick at a crime scene or at an autopsy, and he hoped this wouldn't be the first time. He swallowed hard and turned towards a window to see if he could open it for fresh air. The odours in the place now seemed worse than when he first entered. He felt as though if he didn't get sick he would at least suffocate from the foul air. The window was stuck.

'I'd better be going now, Jean-Pierre,' was all he could manage to say as he quickly exited the room.

'*À bientôt*, Henri.' Ménager's words trailed after him.

Chapter Five

The apartment at 13 rue de Buci seemed sombre and quiet in the pre-dawn hours. Michelet did not come out to greet him. As Corbet entered his kitchen, the copper pots and kitchen utensils looked like macabre weapons ready for battle. He flipped on the light, went to the refrigerator and poured himself a glass of mineral water. He needed something pure to help settle his stomach. The walk from the Quai de la Rapée had helped. Maybe with a bath and a nap he could regain his equilibrium.

As he removed the cuff links from his new custom-made shirt, the image of Marie appeared in his mind's eye. Since his reinvolvement with her he had begun to have his shirts custom-made and to wear cuff links. It made him feel more elegant, more suitable perhaps for her.

She had been so radiant at the soirée last night. One would have thought it was a party in celebration of her triumph. He didn't look forward to telling her about what had happened. He wondered whether he should cancel their luncheon date this afternoon. He would need to be available at the Préfecture. Jouvet would want to see him, Sunday notwithstanding.

He decided he would keep the appointment with Marie if she would agree to making it a bit earlier. He would telephone when he woke up from his nap. He dove into the large sleigh bed and slid under the duvet. Michelet woke up, yawned, stretched and cuddled close to Corbet's large body.

Chapter Six

Le Cochon Doré is a restaurant in Les Halles, the old market district of Paris. It used to be frequented at all hours by vegetable sellers and market men. Now it is part of a group of restaurants owned by the Boulangers. Since Corbet's father was a close friend of and counsel to the head of that family, for years the young Corbet had come to the restaurants which included Le Cochon Doré as well as Au Pied de Voltaire, and La Maison de Choucroute. Le Cochon Doré had become a favourite of his because it was one of the few brasseries in Paris that still remained open all night.

Marie had agreed to meet him there at noon instead of the earlier agreed upon time of two. François, the maitre d' on that shift, greeted Corbet and led them to their table which was at the end of a long, red velveteen banquette. Marie took the banquette side, and Corbet sat in the chair facing her. She was elegantly dressed in a simple hunter green wool suit graced with a silk scarf of just the right shades of green and salmon to complement not only the suit but also her colouring. Corbet was always a bit surprised by her radiance.

'You look lovely.' He took her hand, and she smiled warmly at him.

'Oh, Henri, wasn't it just a wonderful evening? Everything about it was perfect. Your meal will be talked about for a long time.' She picked up the menu and began to examine its offerings.

'Yes, Marie.' He swallowed hard and decided to dive right in with the bad news. 'I'm afraid the evening ended rather badly, though.' He looked at her for a moment.

'Well, what do you mean, Henri? What do you mean?'

'After I dropped you off in the cab, I went home and was just settling in when I got a call from Gilet. They had been summoned to the Maison de Balzac to investigate the death of Véronique Lefèvre. She was found in Balzac's writing room.' He continued to hold her hand and felt her fingers tighten. Her face blanched. He knew that the news he was giving her was all the more upsetting because of her loss of Roger Albert.

'Well, what happened? How did she die?' Her voice shook a bit.

'We're trying to find that out. Ménager is working on it now. As a matter of fact, I visited him early this morning and nearly got sick. I haven't eaten anything yet today. Just thinking of it threatens to ruin my appetite.' Marie's expression acknowledged that she knew that when Corbet's appetite was in jeopardy, it was a serious matter. 'As soon as I have a report, I'll let you know. I've got to see Jouvet this afternoon, and I don't look forward to that.'

'Everyone seemed so happy last night. It was such a joyous occasion. Really, for the first time since I lost Roger I began to genuinely enjoy myself.' Marie lowered her eyes as if to express latent guilt over her indulgence.

'Yes, you looked radiant and very happy.' Corbet smiled at her.

'I did notice that of all the people there Véronique looked the least happy, but most of all she looked as though she were ill. I wondered whether she hadn't been stricken with a serious illness and hadn't yet made a public announcement. I even went so far as to ask Monique about it. She informed me that she was just run down and still grieving over the loss of Raymond. It was obvious that she had been drinking quite a bit.' Marie frowned and seemed to try to recapture the image of Véronique Lefèvre.

The waiter appeared to take their orders. Corbet glanced around him and saw that people were eating a variety of dishes. Several of them looked as though they had large pieces of an animal on their plates, and, in fact, they did. The speciality of the house was a huge serving of braised pigs' feet.

He decided on the petit menu which consisted of a bowl of Le Cochon Doré's famous onion soup and a generous piece of broiled salmon with sorrel purée. That would be gentle enough for his somewhat tentative stomach. He ordered sparkling mineral water, a testament to his need for purification.

Marie considered the braised pigs' feet. She often would eat them when she came here, but today she decided to follow Corbet's example of lighter fare. In spite of his gourmandising, Henri Corbet had not yet been able to eat a pig's foot. Today he doubted that he ever would.

'Marie, you must tell me all you know about Monique de La Tour and her family, everything you know about Véronique Lefèvre. I know Monique is a very good friend of yours. How well did you know Véronique?'

The waiter brought the onion soup. The steam escaped through the melted cheese cover wafting the odour of sweet cooked onions into Corbet's nostrils. He felt his stomach give a little lurch of joy, the kind of sensation he always felt before enjoying a good meal. He took his first bite of the stringy cheese and bread topping. Its mellow taste warmed his mouth and the anticipation of the sweet onions in the hearty broth lifted his spirits.

'I didn't really know her in person. I really only knew of her. At first it was through her articles in *Le Monde*. Everyone in the academic world knew of her in some way. When her book on Beckett came out, of course, it was a great hit, and everyone was reading it and talking about it. I knew of her and knew her indirectly through Monique.

'As you know, Monique and I did graduate work together at the Sorbonne. We also taught in the Bryn Mawr summer program in Avignon. That's when we became really friendly. When I first read her material, I knew she would become somebody very important in Balzac studies. She had always seemed to live in her sister's shadow. That often happens when an older sibling is very gifted and well-known. Monique seemed very graceful about it, though. I never detected any resentment on her part. She was so disciplined in her work. She had been involved in the project on Balzac and the creative process for a number of years. I was delighted when she finally published her book and got the recognition she deserved. She never mentioned Véronique's reaction to it.' Marie began to eat her onion soup.

'Oh, Henri, this is wonderful as usual.' Corbet smiled at her as he swallowed a rich, mellow spoonful of the onions and broth.

'Yes, quite good.' He was relieved to have his stomach back on speaking terms with his enjoyment of food. 'What about that son, Raymond? Died a couple of years ago? Committed suicide?' He finished the last drop of his soup.

'Oh, yes, Raymond. Monique was terribly fond of him. That was a rather sad story. Apparently Véronique abandoned him when he was very young. She just didn't want to take care of a child. He began spending more and more time with Monique. He moved in with her when he was about five years old. By then Georges and Véronique were separated, and it looked as though their marriage would soon be over for good. The whole family thought it best that Raymond remain with Monique. Véronique went on to put all of her energy into her career and her rather depraved love life. According to Monique, she had had a number of unhappy love affairs and never could resist the challenge of an attractive man. The only thing that seemed to work in her life was her career.' Marie had now finished her soup. The waiter brought the salmon.

'And Monique?' Corbet took his first bite of the broiled salmon which he had garnished with a dollop of the sorrel purée. The joyous symphony of flavours burst in his mouth, green, smoky and soft. He smiled at Marie and waited for her reply.

'In spite of the fact that she's a good friend of mine, I feel I can be objective. Monique was a much more balanced person. She was very devoted to her work, but she also took great care with her personal relationships. She nurtured them, treasured them.

'She was a wonderful parent to Raymond. She was always very concerned about his welfare, spent a lot of time with him and encouraged his talent. He showed great academic potential. She guided him. He attended the Sorbonne for a couple of years, but then he decided to become a novice. He joined an order down in Avignon but left after two years. Although the high ritual of the church appealed to his aesthetic sense, the actual day-to-day life was too confining for him, really, too ascetic. He decided that his real vocation was writing. He began to write and supported himself with odd jobs and contributions from his family.

'Monique was very generous with him, and Véronique would not be outdone by her even though she didn't really believe in his talent. She never hesitated to underline her lack of confidence when she delivered her contributions to his livelihood.' Marie paused to take a bite of her salmon.

'I understand he had published a novel which had won him some recognition even among the more pedantic critics?' Corbet was savouring the last bites of his salmon.

'Yes. It was called *Beyond the Night*. It's the story of a young man's spiritual odyssey, a fictionalised account of his own struggle. When he became known in the literary world, Véronique began to come around. She actually told him she liked the book. Of course, she couldn't review it because of their blood ties.' Marie sighed and took a long drink of mineral water.

'That was probably just as well for Raymond,' Corbet couldn't help adding. He began to think about dessert. Glancing at the card, he noticed that they were offering crème caramel. That would be another soother for his recovering stomach. The waiter arrived and took their dishes and their orders. Marie decided to join him in the crème caramel. Corbet hesitated to ask for the coffee he was beginning to feel the need of and instead took tisane. It would fight less directly with his stomach.

'Raymond had also met a woman while he was in Avignon. He may have met her when he was still in the priesthood which must have made for an interesting struggle. At least something like that happens in his book. At any rate, her name is Blanche Ballard, and he lived with her right up until he died. She was quite a bit older and seemed to offer him the stability he needed. According to Monique, he made great creative strides during his time with her. Of course, this didn't go over too well with Véronique. She wanted to mend fences with her son who was not only a published but also a well-recognised author. Blanche, on the other hand, had no use for Véronique whom she never could forgive for her earlier neglect of Raymond.'

'And Monique?' Corbet waited.

'Monique was caught somewhat in the middle. She was glad for Raymond's sake that at last his mother showed some interest in him, but she couldn't forget the scars she had inflicted on him by her neglect.' The crème caramel arrived and Marie picked up her spoon to sample it.

'So Raymond's ultimate response to all of this was to kill himself?' Corbet let his first spoonful of the custard melt to the back of his mouth.

'Well, yes, I guess you could put it that way. Even in his most successful and apparently happy moments, there was always a dark side to Raymond, according to Monique. She talked to me a lot about him right after he died. She was devastated. She used to say that charming and kind though he was she could always sense something brooding in the background. She had comforted herself with the idea that it would pass with time and more success, but it didn't.' Marie looked into Corbet's large, brown eyes. Her eyes filled with tears. Corbet took her hand and cupped it in both of his. He only needed for the moment to inquire a bit further about Véronique, and then he would happily let Marie rest and finish her dessert.

'Just a bit more, Marie.' He continued to hold her hand. 'What about Véronique? It appears she took his death pretty hard?' Corbet locked eyes again with Marie.

'Yes, she did. According to Monique, it seemed to push Véronique over the edge in her own personal crisis. She began to drink very heavily and to rely on large quantities of drugs to cope with her life.' Corbet released Marie's hand and took the last two bites of his custard.

'Which explains the state she was in when she died.' He decided not to mention the Balzac quotations found at the scene until he knew the source of the handwriting. Corbet savoured the last of his custard. His stomach was welcoming the soothing substance. He was feeling better now, but he had to fight with his imagination not to reproduce images of the scene at the laboratory with Ménager.

'Marie, thanks so much. You've given me a lot to think about. Now I just have to get by Jouvet and that nest of snakes that is the current politics of the Préfecture. This will be a hard one, I'm afraid.' Marie gazed at him sympathetically responding to his need for reassurance.

'Henri, you will triumph as always, I'm sure.' She beamed her support to him through her warm smile. It hit the target, and Corbet felt his spirit as soothed by it as his stomach had been by the food.

Chapter Seven

The Paris Préfecture de Police crouched on the Quai des Orfèvres, a hulking, grey cat stalking its prey in the mud-brown ribbon of the Seine. The quiet Sunday afternoon had the ominous and portentous quality of midnight as Inspector Henri Corbet mounted the steps and entered the very silent grand hall. Jouvet was waiting for him. He took a deep breath and drew some reassurance from his full and now quiet stomach. He headed down the long, narrow hallway to the large door with the letters indicating that it was the office of Commissioner Jouvet. He knocked even though the door was slightly ajar.

'Come in,' a grand voice boomed from behind the glass. Corbet entered the room to find Commissioner Jouvet seated very properly behind his desk. He was a narrow, straight man with what Corbet felt must be perfect posture. His thinning hair was neatly combed and distributed over his head in an attempt to hide the fact that he was balding. Corbet noticed this and felt glad for his full head of silver-gold hair.

'Ah, Corbet. You've gotten yourself into quite a tangle, I see.' Jouvet grinned. He reminded Corbet of a great, scrawny cat with bad teeth.

'If you're referring to the Véronique Lefèvre case, yes, I'm now involved in that.' Corbet needed to play close to the vest with this man. He knew he would try to torment him into some sort of an overreaction, evidence of his inability to be impartial.

'I've been giving this situation a great deal of thought.' Jouvet licked his lips, savouring the morsel of his power over Corbet. 'I wonder if you aren't too close to the case. You were at the soirée where the murder took place. You're acquainted with people who know the parties. Maybe you're too close?' Again he grinned at him like a cat enjoying the opportunity to torment its prey.

'My only real personal connection with the people involved is Marie Marceau.' Corbet would stick strictly to the facts.

'Yes, Marie Marceau, that woman you've become involved with as a result of the Albert and de La Roche cases.' He had out the hook. 'Really, Corbet, I don't think this will do.' Corbet was glad that Jouvet didn't know that in fact he had known Marie a long time before the Albert case. He felt himself begin to lurch to a defence of his relationship with her but decided not to take the bait.

'Anyway, it seems that this case is more suited to Renard than to you, your first-hand knowledge of the parties notwithstanding.' The hook had gone in. Corbet sat stunned for a moment as though waiting for the blood to begin to run.

'Why is that so, Commissioner?' He had to take the bait now. It didn't go down well.

'Well, it seems to me that his method is more suited to it. His orderly and formal approach to the investigation and solution of crimes is what won him such recognition for the Tissot case. This case, as I see it, is both a hard evidence and a psychological one.' He grinned at Corbet.

'All the more reason to let me stay with it, Commissioner,' Corbet challenged him.

'Yes, Corbet. I know all about your great and often good use of your intuition when solving a case, but this is one where I'm afraid the fact that you know at least one of the parties very well may cloud your judgement.' He lit a cigarette and blew the smoke in Corbet's direction. Corbet recoiled a bit. He detested the smell of cigarette smoke. It made him feel as though he were being poisoned. It was hard now not to rise to the bait about Marie.

'I assure you, Commissioner, that I will be able to use all of my faculties in solving this murder just as I have in many others, just as I did in the de La Roche and Albert cases.' This was as close as he could come to a defence of his relationship with Marie.

'Well, I have grave doubts. I want you to know that, grave doubts.' Jouvet took a deep drag on his cigarette and seemed to stare off into space. Corbet sat silently. 'I'm under a great deal of pressure from people in high places, from the Society of the Friends of Honoré de Balzac, in particular, to solve this crime. I'll have you know that I'll be watching you very carefully throughout this investigation.' He punctuated the sombre threat with a large sigh. 'If I feel at any point that my instincts are bearing me out, I'll remove you immediately.' He glared at Corbet.

'Of course, Commissioner,' was all Corbet could manage to say.

'Any leads?' Corbet knew that the intense supervision was just beginning.

'Well, Ménager is working on the body. He thinks it's some kind of induced cardiac arrest. The hard evidence team has combed the crime scene and are at work now. I've begun to gather background on the victim and those close to her. I'll meet with Gilet tonight to set out our strategy. Leroux, of course, will be on hand.'

'You know you might benefit from a consult with Renard about the case at some point?' He finished the question with a raise of his thin eyebrows. 'He's awfully good at not missing any detail.' He was wiggling the hook.

'If I feel the need, I'll do so.' Corbet didn't want to refuse outright. He felt that any direct confrontation now would be damaging to him. With the promotion on the line, he had to go gently.

'Well, Corbet, as I said before, I have my doubts.' Jouvet reached for another cigarette, lit it and blew the smoke at Corbet who stood to prepare to make his exit.

'Don't get all muddled up with these people, Corbet.' He blew a trail of smoke after Corbet who was making his way to the door.

'I'll do my best, Commissioner, as I always do.'

Chapter Eight

Corbet pulled his coat tighter around his large frame and hurried down the rue du Pont Neuf. It was already dark, the streets were deserted, and a light rain had begun to fall. He was meeting Gilet for dinner at Au Chien qui Fume, a bistro specialising in seafood in the heart of Les Halles. Corbet had heard that an owner, who had taken charge of the bistro in the twenties, had given pipes to his dogs. The story goes that the animals had smoked them to the amusement of the customers. Today the place is covered with pictures and statues of canines.

'Inspector Corbet, good evening.' Jean, the maitre d', knew Corbet well and ushered him to a table by the window. Corbet let him know he was waiting for Gilet and ordered an apéritif. His stomach seemed to have made a full recovery, and he was contemplating a large portion of raw Breton oysters to start things off. They were having a special, all the oysters one could eat for a fixed price. That was tempting, but he knew that he often didn't know when to stop eating the delicate little creatures. Maybe Gilet would assist him.

He looked up to find Gilet's lanky form rushing towards him. 'Ah, Inspector, sorry I'm late. My wife had some relatives over for a Sunday afternoon meal, and she had a lot of things for me to do. I'm glad to get away. It gets too confusing with all of those people.' Gilet sat down opposite Corbet and picked up the menu that Jean had left there for him. 'I want something light.' Corbet proposed an oyster share, and Gilet agreed. Corbet also ordered an endive and roquefort salad and a bottle of Sauvignon Blanc.

'Ménager says she was given an overdose of digitoxin which led to cardiac arrest. He also found that she was poisoning herself with barbiturates and alcohol. It didn't take much to push her over the edge.'

'What about the cup with the lipstick?' Gilet removed his large elbows from the table as the waiter brought the salad and the mountain of raw oysters accompanied by a red wine vinegar and shallot dip and small slices of dark rye bread and butter.

'It matched the lipstick left on her lips. She had been drinking coffee out of the Limoges cup into which somebody had put liquid digitoxin. It went to work immediately.' Gilet began to attack the oysters.

'Take these and find out whose handwriting they're in.' Corbet reached into his jacket pocket and took out the two wrinkled pieces of paper with the handwritten quotations on them. Get samples of the handwriting of all of those close to Véronique Lefèvre.' Corbet finished his salad and reached for the oysters.

'Will do, Inspector.' Gilet smiled showing his large even teeth.

Corbet helped himself to a shiny, grey oyster, first covering it with the vinegar and shallot mixture and then lifting it to his mouth on the end of a small fork. The briny, sharp taste of the oyster set off by the somewhat tart yet mellow taste of the vinegar and shallots made him glad that his stomach was back in form. As he swallowed the oyster and savoured the piquant taste, he wondered whether Véronique Lefèvre had tasted anything when she had swallowed the coffee with digitoxin. He dismissed the thought with the idea that her consumption of alcohol and barbiturates had probably numbed her tastebuds. He would check that out with Ménager.

'Any ideas?' Gilet dove into the oysters and began to eat one after the other, first covering them with the sauce and then following with a bite of the dark rye bread and butter. Corbet watched him.

'Didn't they feed you at home today?' Corbet couldn't help asking.

'Well, you see, my wife likes to feed these people all the things I don't like – rich pâtés made of rabbit and goose liver – and I really didn't eat much today, no.' He popped another oyster into his mouth.

'It's a good thing we can have all we want, because I feel like a good oyster feed myself tonight. I haven't been feeling too well today. I had the unfortunate experience of watching Ménager perform part of the autopsy. My stomach has been in revolt all day. I've just begun to recover.' Inspector Corbet downed another oyster followed by a good swallow of the Sauvignon Blanc.

'Any ideas?' Gilet repeated his prior question.

'Well, I've only talked with Henriette and Marie. Marie knows the family quite well. Monique de La Tour is a good friend of hers. She says that Véronique Lefèvre had been in decline for some time, but severely so since the death of her son. Rumour has it he committed suicide. I'll need to look into that.' Corbet paused and sighed deeply.

'This appears to be another of those twisted family tangles that so often lead to murder.' He swallowed another oyster. 'I'm not exactly sure where to start, but I think I'll do what I always do in cases like this, look to the nearest relatives. That would be her ex-husband, George Lefèvre, and her sister, Monique. There's also the son's girlfriend, Blanche Ballard. We can take a look at her, too. I'll start with the ex-husband. Ex-husbands often have lingering axes to grind with ex-wives. You can start with Monique de La Tour. I'll put Leroux on Blanche Ballard and some of the people at the soirée.'

Corbet looked quizzically at Gilet as he reached for the last oyster on the emptied plate. Gilet nodded the go ahead, and Corbet popped the little, grey creature into his mouth.

'I'm going to need a lot of help from you and Leroux on this one. Jouvet is going to be breathing down my neck, watching every move I make. He's getting a lot of pressure from people in high places to solve the murder quickly. He thinks I'm too closely associated with the people involved to be effective. I need to prove him wrong, and I don't think he's going to make that easy for me. He'll also be shoving Renard down my throat at every turn.' Corbet drained his glass.

'Yes, Inspector, you can certainly count on us. I know I can speak for Leroux. Renard is not to be believed. He's so arrogant and so ignorant. We don't want to have to work with him as Chief Inspector. We're in your corner, Inspector.' Gilet smiled and patted Corbet on the arm. 'We're with you.'

'I hope so. Don't forget the choucroute at my place tomorrow night.' Corbet motioned for the waiter, 'The bill, please.'

'I won't, and I'm sure Leroux won't eat all day so he can better enjoy the feast.' Corbet paid the bill and left Gilet to head home to get some sleep. He would talk with Georges Lefèvre first thing in the morning.

Chapter Nine

Inspector Corbet eagerly approached his nineteenth-century copper bathtub which was filled with hot, steaming water. As he let himself gently down into the warm liquid, he could feel his whole body begin to relax. Whenever he could, he tried to take a long morning bath to prepare himself for whatever the day might hold.

He leaned back in the tub and began to contemplate the day ahead starting with the breakfast he would prepare when he finished his soak. His stomach had made a full recovery and eagerly awaited the fresh orange juice, homemade croissants and strong coffee.

He wondered what he would find out in his interview with Georges Lefèvre. He had heard of the man before this incident and not through Marie. Corbet had known him as the owner and publisher of a newspaper called *Le Journal d'aujourd'hui*, a tabloid with little to recommend it over *Le Monde*. All the news that was sensational to print one found on the front pages of *Le Journal* without much effort on the part of the journalists to digest and interpret. The strength of the paper seemed to be in the ability of its reporters to get word of every seamy activity from sources and informants in all of the sewers of Paris.

Corbet didn't really look forward to meeting Lefèvre. He had seen him Saturday night at the party at the Maison de Balzac but had not really talked to him. He hated to think about what his paper was going to do with the murder of its owner's ex-wife. He felt a sudden chill, shivered and turned on the hot water once again to heat up his bath. It was difficult to keep it hot enough. Finally, when he felt warmed through, he got up and dried himself off and headed for the bedroom to dress.

Chapter Ten

The rue du Bac was not crowded at this time of the morning as Corbet rushed down the street to the offices of *Le Journal* where he hoped to find Georges Lefèvre. He found him in a second floor suite in the rear of the building. He was led into the office by a young gentleman who had a desk just outside.

As he entered the door the lanky, grey-haired Lefèvre headed towards him with his hand extended. Corbet shook his hand without much enthusiasm and took the chair he was offered. His eye took in the room, and he was quite astounded at the good taste in which it was furnished with an eclectic mix of antique furniture and two floor-to-ceiling bookcases full of leather-bound volumes. The titles were at such a distance that he couldn't make them out, but the bindings looked impressive.

'Yes, Inspector, I was wondering when you would come.' Georges Lefèvre was a very tall man with collar-length, grey hair and light blue eyes. His grey, silk suit was not a style that particularly appealed to Corbet. The patent leather shoes that Corbet had noticed on his feet before he sat down summed up the look as slick and stylish, that of a mannequin in an old-world setting.

'Well, Monsieur Lefèvre, please accept my condolences on the loss of your ex-wife, if condolences are in order.'

'I'm not sure they are, Inspector. You see, Véronique and I were not exactly on the best of terms, particularly of late.' Lefèvre reached for a gold cigarette box on the mahogany table, opened it, took out a cigarette and held the box out to Inspector Corbet.

'No, thank you. I don't smoke.' Corbet instinctively leaned back in his chair and waited for the onslaught of the sulphur and smoke that would come from the lighting of the cigarette. 'Well, I know you've been divorced from her for some time. How long is it now?' Corbet turned his head to the side to avoid the on-coming smoke.

'Actually, we were never formally divorced, but we have been separated for well over twenty years now. It's hard to believe that so much time has gone by, and, yet, it was truly another world when I lived with Véronique.' Lefèvre took a long drag on his cigarette.

'How do you mean another world?' Corbet couldn't resist.

'Well, I feel I was a very different person then. I was a struggling young journalist, and she was already established in her academic career and had just begun writing for *Le Monde.* She didn't want children, and, so, when our son was born, she all but abandoned him, leaving much of his care to me. I loved him dearly, but it was hard for me because I needed to spend so much time getting my career off the ground. If Monique hadn't stepped in, I don't know what we would have done. She virtually became his mother.' Lefèvre got up from his chair and went over to a silver tray with a decanter and some glasses. 'Cognac?' he inquired.

'No, not this early.' Corbet waited. He liked to give people as much free reign as possible when he began his questioning.

'Our marriage had begun to fall apart, however, even before the birth of Raymond. We were very different people. In looking back now, I wonder how it was that we ever got together in the first place. It was one of those flash-in-the pan, intense attractions that seem very destined at the time but which are based on such illusion that they pale quickly in the strong light of continued exposure. I guess that's what happened to us.'

Lefèvre took a large swig of Cognac and sat down again. 'I often wonder what would have become of me if I had stayed married to her. At the beginning I had loftier ambitions in the field of journalism, more along the lines of *Le Monde*. However, my talent seemed to lie in another direction.' He watched Corbet who found the use of the word *talent* in this context a bit surprising. Lefèvre read his expression.

'Yes, I said *talent*. I do think that it takes a certain ability not only to follow one's nose into the sewer, but then to be able to trap and expose the source of the odour.' He took another large swig of Cognac.

'How did Véronique feel about your journalistic leanings?' Corbet asked the question knowing the answer.

'Well, that's not too hard to figure out, Inspector. She thought my teaming up with *Le Journal* was professional suicide. When I took the job it sounded the death knell of our marriage.' He stared off into space and appeared to be waiting for the next question.

'If your career had taken another turn, do you think the marriage would have survived?' Corbet didn't know the answer to that one.

'Actually, no. The level of emotional incompatibility was as great as the disparity between her lofty critical aspirations and my more mundane and sensational leanings. We were a sadly mismatched pair, I'm afraid.' He got up and went to the decanter to refill his glass with more Cognac. It always amazed Corbet how some people could drink so heavily in the morning. Lunch was the earliest he could even begin to think about consuming alcohol.

'What has been the nature of your relationship with her since the separation? I know that's going back a long way.' Corbet waited.

'Well, I guess you could say that the incompatibility did nothing but deepen. The more famous she became as a critic for *Le Monde* and the more well-known I became as a contributor to and the eventual owner of *Le Journal*, the more divergent our paths. We were still linked, of course, by Raymond while he was alive. However, it wasn't until his book became a success that she really seemed to want to have anything to do with him. Then she took notice of him. She was a cold and heartless woman.' He closed his mouth firmly and stared into space.

'How frequently did you see her or have anything to do with her?' Corbet wished he could have a glass of water. His mouth was getting dry.

'As little as possible. Concerning Raymond, I dealt mostly with Monique. She was the softer more gentle of the two. I hate to think of what Raymond would have grown up to be if she hadn't taken him under her wing. It's impossible to believe that a mother could abandon her own child.' He again stopped and stared into space. It was as though in saying these words out loud and defining the character of his dead wife he was seeing it clearly for the first time.

'Were you surprised when he committed suicide?'

'If that's what really happened. I have my doubts about that, Inspector. I think Raymond had been healing from the wounds of his childhood and that the success of his book and the fact that he had found his calling at last are pretty strong evidence against his having committed suicide. I know that the police were apparently satisfied that that was what it was, but I've always had my doubts.'

The phone on Lefèvre's desk gave a loud ring, and he picked it up. 'Tell him I'll meet him later this afternoon. No, I don't want to be disturbed now.' He hung up the receiver and looked directly at Corbet who wondered how an apparently articulate and insightful man like Lefèvre could have ended up at the head of a newspaper like *Le Journal*.

'Were you close to Raymond?' The direct question was always the best.

'Well, closer than his mother was. I was, of course, very busy when he was growing up and could in no way take the place of a mother, but I always tried to spend as much time as I could with him, took him to art exhibitions, encouraged his academic studies, things like that. He was a very good student, you know. He did honours level work at the Sorbonne. Word has it that he was the real genius in the family, the creative genius. I think that Véronique knew this and resented him for it. She had to be the centre of attention at all times.' The bitter tone of his delivery jarred Corbet who blinked and made a mental note of it.

'You really didn't like her much, did you?' Corbet couldn't resist the obvious.

'I think you could safely say I despised her, Inspector.' Lefèvre took a long swill of Cognac and plunked his glass squarely down on the desk. 'I hope you're nearing the end of your inquiry. I have a lot of work to do today, and I've already gotten a rather late start.' He looked directly at Corbet, and then he got up and began to walk around the room as though trying to free himself from some disturbing picture or thought.

'My intense dislike of her, however, Inspector, did not lead me to kill her.' Lefèvre stopped his pacing about ten feet away from Corbet's chair. He just stood there and waited.

'We always need to start with the closest relatives, Monsieur Lefèvre. When we first started talking you said that it was particularly of late that you were having difficulty with Véronique. Why was that?' Corbet waited.

'Well, you see, Inspector, even though we had lived apart for enough years that she couldn't effectively oppose a divorce, I never pressed for one. I knew that if she thought I wanted one she would take great joy in making my life miserable. I was also concerned that she might become even more vicious towards Raymond. He had suffered enough. I had hoped that eventually she would come to want a divorce and make it easy for me. That never happened. It wasn't until recently when I began to have a serious relationship that I asked Véronique for a divorce. Of course, when she discovered that the woman I wished to marry was none other than Blanche Ballard, Raymond's former girlfriend, she was furious. Every encounter from then on was more difficult than it had been at the very beginning of the separation.' Lefèvre rose again to pour himself yet another Cognac.

'How tangled,' was all Corbet could manage as he tried to digest this new information. 'I hope your paper won't sensationalise this murder so much that it interferes with our finding the killer.' Corbet eyes followed Lefèvre who went back to the desk.

'I've given reporters the word to play it down. Of course, we have to report something about it. When every other newspaper in Paris is running stories on the death of Véronique Lefèvre, we can't be completely silent. I'm sure you understand, Inspector.' Corbet did.

'Now, Monsieur Lefèvre, I'm afraid I must ask you some very specific questions about your actions at the soirée at the Maison de Balzac the night that Véronique Lefèvre was murdered.' Corbet eyed Lefèvre who seated himself again behind his desk and waited.

'Go ahead, Inspector.' He took a long swig of Cognac.

'I know you were in attendance because I remember seeing you there. Can you give me a general outline of your movements that night?'

'Well, needless to say, I wasn't very comfortable that evening. I only went because I knew that Monique would never forgive me if I didn't show up. In fact, I was supposed to go to the soirée with her but decided against it in order not to further activate Véronique's resentment. I went to the soirée by myself. Blanche and I didn't go as a couple and didn't behave as though we were a couple while we were there. I just circulated and talked with some of the people I know in the publishing world.

'At one point, Blanche came up to me and indicated that she wanted to leave early and asked me to meet her outside of the Maison de Balzac. I said I thought we shouldn't do that. She insisted, but I told her I would meet her later at her place, which I did.' Lefèvre sighed and lit another cigarette and slowly blew out the smoke as he waited for further questions.

'Henriette, the housekeeper and cook at the Maison de Balzac, said that Blanche was pestering her husband to let her leave by the secret door Balzac used to escape his creditors. Did Blanche mention anything about that to you?' Corbet again leaned back to avoid the smoke.

'Yes, she had mentioned that she was going to be let out by the secret back door. I told her to go ahead, that I would meet her later. As far as I know, she left then.'

'And what time would that have been, if you know?'

'Around ten o'clock. I remember looking at my watch. I waited a bit and then left myself. That's all I can tell you, Inspector. That and that I didn't kill my wife.' He looked at Corbet with tired and determined eyes.

'Well, I think that'll be it for now. I'll be in touch when I need to talk to you again.' Corbet rose and reached for the hand that Lefèvre extended across the desk.

'Good day, Inspector. Martin will show you out.' He buzzed for the young man who entered and led Corbet out of the room.

Chapter Eleven

Inspector Corbet moved at a quick pace down the rue de Buci towards the Alsatian charcuterie located across the street from his apartment. As he entered the shop, the aroma of sauerkraut and smoked meats greeted him like an old friend. The scent took him back to the days he had spent as a teenager at his grandfather Corbet's house in Strasbourg. The elder Corbet had loved to cook, and several times a winter Henri Corbet would be treated to his choucroute garnie. The young Corbet had stood by eagerly and watched his grandfather make the bountiful, hearty dish of specially prepared sauerkraut and smoked meats. Now, almost as if in memory of him, at least once a year, usually during early January, Corbet made his own large portion of choucroute garnie in the huge copper stockpot he had inherited from him.

'Hello, Mimi. It's choucroute garnie time again.' Corbet rubbed his hands together and began to actively inspect the array of smoked meats and sauerkraut. 'I'll need about six pounds of sauerkraut.' He didn't tell Mimi that he would then proceed to doctor the house sauerkraut before beginning to prepare the dish. That was one of his little secrets.

'Yes, and two pounds each of pork shoulder and loin. Ah, yes, and a pound of slab bacon, a pound of salt pork, and a couple of pounds of frankfurters and knackwurst. And, of course, the pig's knuckles, two pounds.' Corbet paused a minute to run through the recipe in his mind. 'Yes, I think that will do.' He had already purchased the other ingredients: the wine, the spices, herbs and potatoes, and he had his own supply of the essential goose fat.

'Will that be all, Inspector?' Mimi watched him warmly, seeming to enjoy his delight in purchasing the makings of a feast.

'Yes, Mimi. Thanks so much. *À très bientôt.*' Corbet exited the shop and hurried across the street and up into his warm apartment to begin his creation. As he entered the hallway, he was greeted by a rather assertive Michelet who followed him into the kitchen trying to rub around his legs as he moved. Corbet put the bundles on the kitchen table and proceeded to put away the ingredients he had just purchased.

First he would have to make the choucroute, prepare the sauerkraut to be used in the dish. He went over to his pantry cupboard and took out a large, cast iron pot into which he put all six pounds of the sauerkraut with enough water to cover it. After letting it soak for ten minutes, he drained the kraut in a colander and began to melt goose fat in the cast iron kettle. To the melted fat he added a good quantity of sliced onions and minced garlic, stirred them around and waited until they wilted. He then added the rinsed sauerkraut, some Riesling, chicken broth, and a bouquet garni of parsley, thyme, bay leaf, cloves and juniper berries. Once the mixture was seasoned with salt and pepper, it would be brought to the boil and then simmered for twenty minutes.

With the sauerkraut under way, Corbet began to assemble the meats for the garnie. He wanted to get everything prepared and in the oven so that he could have time for a nap before Gilet and Leroux arrived. They both had been away from the Préfecture all day, and he was eager to hear what they would report to him about their respective interviews with Monique de La Tour and Blanche Ballard.

He thought about his encounter with Georges Lefèvre. The man appeared to be the soul of incongruity. Indeed, he had a strong motive for wanting to get rid of his wife. He was at the scene of the crime and could probably have gotten hold of the deadly dose of digitoxin. The acrimony between him and Véronique alone might have been motive enough, let alone the fact that he now wanted to marry his son's former girlfriend. It was even a stretch for Corbet to believe in the coincidence of Lefèvre's falling in love with Blanche. He could only imagine how this appeared to an estranged wife who was bitter and paranoid to begin with.

The sharp, spicy smell of the cooking sauerkraut brought him back to the task at hand. Lifting the cover of the pot and letting the full strength of the cooked mixture hit his nostrils, Corbet prepared to drain the sauerkraut before mixing it with the smoked meats. Having drained it, he left the steaming mass in the colander while he retrieved his large copper stockpot. Into the bottom of his heirloom he melted some goose fat and sautéed a large quantity of sliced onions until they were wilted but not browned. He then added a full bottle of Riesling and half of the sauerkraut and blended the mixture well before adding the smoked shoulder, the pork loin, the bacon, the salt pork, and the pig's knuckles. To this he added enough water to cover, a bouquet garni of coriander seeds, juniper berries, cumin seeds, whole cloves, bay leaves and peppercorns. On top of this he added the remaining sauerkraut. He brought the large mixture to the boil and then put it in the oven to cook for an hour and a half during which time he would take a well-deserved nap with Michelet snuggling at his side.

Inspector Corbet fell into a somewhat troubled but heavy sleep. He was aware of having one of those dreams where he was being pursued, he didn't know by whom or why, only that the person or thing was menacing. After tossing and turning for about an hour, he awoke not to the sound of his alarm, but rather to the smell of his cooking creation. The odours of the kraut, spices, wine and smoked meats permeated the apartment and reached his grateful nostrils. He stirred himself and got up to put the finishing touches on his meal.

About forty-five minutes later the buzzer rang, and Inspector Corbet let in the bulky Leroux whose face beamed with anticipation as the scent of the upcoming feast greeted him. He had no sooner provided Leroux with an apéritif when the buzzer rang again, and Corbet admitted the lanky Gilet who proudly announced that he had eaten very lightly at lunch so that he would have the appetite that he knew Corbet's dinner deserved.

Settled in his living room on his antique black leather sofas with his two assistants, drinks in hand, surrounded by the heavenly aroma of the choucroute garnie, Inspector Corbet wished momentarily that this were merely a social occasion and that there were no deadly matters on the agenda. For a brief moment, he considered the possibility of waiting until morning to discuss business with his assistants. The idea was quickly overridden by the necessity to pursue the case at hand as well as his frank curiosity about what they had learned from Blanche Ballard and Monique de La Tour. He would at least wait before bringing up the topics until the meal was served and his guests had had an opportunity to enjoy the first few bites of his masterpiece.

The dining-room table was set with some of his mother's Limoges, Lalique crystal and his grandmother's Christofle silver. Corbet had procured some peach-coloured roses from the florist down the street, and these were arranged in a large round bowl in the centre of the table. The lovely flowers matched the peach in the pattern of the

Limoges. The Inspector was delighted with this backdrop for his offering.

From the rather awkward way Gilet and Leroux took their seats and smoothed their linen napkins on their laps, Corbet could tell that it was not very often that they ate a meal in such a sumptuous setting. He noticed Leroux studying the arrangement of the silver as though talking himself through how to use each utensil.

Gilet, always the more at ease of the two, glanced about, smoothed his napkin, and then began to engage Leroux in some light banter about goings-on at the Préfecture. The conversation stopped when Inspector Corbet appeared in the doorway with a large silver platter upon which was arranged his glorious choucroute garnie. The fragrant and steaming creation spoke through the nostrils of wonders to come to the tastebuds.

'Oh, now, Inspector, you've really outdone yourself.' Gilet rubbed his hands together and eagerly watched the progression of the bounty on the silver platter to the centre of the table. Leroux's large, brown eyes seemed transfixed by the magic of his boss's presentation. He looked like a large beagle dog whose master is about to feed him some very tasty morsel.

'Yes, gentlemen, it's my pleasure to prepare this for you. Hand me your plates, and I'll serve you.' The two assistants handed the Inspector their plates like hungry, grateful children. Inspector Corbet dished up huge mounds of the fragrant sauerkraut and topped it with sliced selections of the meats. He served Leroux first because he looked the most uncomfortable. Gilet's long arm extended across half the table to rescue his plate from the extended arm of Inspector Corbet. 'There's mustard, several different kinds – Dijon, horseradish, dark granular. Help yourselves.' Inspector Corbet passed them a round carrier containing five or six small mustard jars.

A reverent silence fell on the room as the three men sampled the bounty before them. Corbet was loath to disrupt the scene of devotion to his efforts.

'Very good. Very good.' The silence was broken by the simple praises of Leroux who eyed the Inspector gratefully.

'Thank you, Leroux. It's my grandfather's version. He used to make this for me when I was young.' Corbet savoured a large portion of sauerkraut and smoked pork. He followed that by lifting his glass to take a drink of the accompanying Riesling.

'To your grandfather,' Gilet raised his glass to the others who in turn raised theirs to him.

'Thank you, Gilet.' Corbet drained his glass and filled it again. 'And now on to the case at hand. Who wants to go first with his report? Why don't you go, Leroux.' Corbet knew if he didn't invite Leroux that Gilet would certainly take centre stage.

'Well, Inspector, I spent part of the afternoon speaking with Blanche Ballard. She claims that she left the murder scene around ten o'clock last night by a secret door in the house. The live-in gardener let her out. Says she wasn't even around when the crime was committed.' Leroux took a small bite of his meal.

'Well, do you believe her?' Corbet knew it would be a bit like pulling teeth to get to Leroux's instinctual reading of the interview, but that it would be worth the effort. Leroux had excellent instincts.

'Yes and no.' Leroux waited for Corbet's next question.

'What part do you believe?'

'Well, I believe that she left when she said she did. I also talked with the gardener. He confirmed her story. Says he let her out the back way at about ten o'clock.'

'What don't you believe about her story?' Corbet looked inquiringly at Leroux.

'Well, it's not what I don't believe about it. It's that I don't think she told me everything. I had the sense that there was much that she was leaving out.'

'It was not what she said, but what she didn't say?' Gilet inquired with a twinkle in his eye.

'You could say that, yes.' Leroux confirmed.

'What was her emotional state?' Corbet finished his wine.

'Well, she didn't really seem upset. She seemed more distracted than anything, as though she had a lot on her mind and was going through the motions with me, telling me what she had to in order to get the interview over with.'

'Were you able to get any sense of what her preoccupation was about?' Corbet glanced at Gilet who was looking hungrily at the platter in the centre of the table. He seemed to want seconds but hesitated to take them or ask for them.

'Help yourself, Gilet.' The invitation hung in the air. Gilet reached across the table, seized the silver platter and began to fill his plate again. Leroux eyed him longingly. 'You, too, Leroux.' Corbet waited.

'Not really, just that she seemed to wander off mentally while I talked to her.' Leroux gratefully accepted the sliver tray from Gilet and began to refill his plate.

'Well, what did you learn about her life, her relationships?' Corbet himself now took the platter and began to refill his plate.

'She said that she had been involved with the son of Véronique Lefèvre, that he had died a couple of years ago.'

'Did she say how he had died?'

'Just that he was supposed to have committed suicide. She said she didn't believe he had. She said she thought he had been murdered.' Leroux looked attentively at Corbet.

'Murdered? Did she say by whom?' Corbet lifted his eyebrows and waited.

'No. Just that she didn't believe the story about his having committed suicide. She seemed angry and quite bitter.'

'What about her reaction to the death of Véronique Lefèvre? Did she seem surprised?' Corbet took a big forkful of sauerkraut.

'She just said that somebody had helped Véronique to do what she was trying to do anyway, kill herself with alcohol and drugs.' Leroux took the last morsel of meat from his plate.

'Did she tell you that she was involved with the estranged husband of Véronique Lefèvre, Georges?' Corbet wondered how much this woman was trying to conceal.

'No, she didn't. That was one of the things that she left out.' Leroux brought his napkin to his mouth and began to pat at the corners signalling that he had completed his meal.

'Anything else of importance you think I should know?'

'Can't think of anything right now, Inspector.' Leroux looked like a child waiting for dessert.

'All right. Before we start with you, Gilet. Let me gather up these plates and serve dessert. We have poached fruit with a Riesling custard sauce. A little something light after our heavy meal.' Corbet gathered up the dishes and brought them to the kitchen. While out there, he assembled the desserts and then brought them in on another silver tray and served them to his guests.

'And, now, Gilet, let's hear from you.' Corbet took a large bite of his custard and fruit. 'What about Monique de La Tour? What was your impression of her?'

'First off, Inspector, the graphologist has determined that the quotations found at the scene were in her handwriting.' Gilet waited for Corbet to absorb the jolt.

'You don't say! Did you confront her with that?'

'I didn't know about it when I talked to her. She's quite an attractive woman. That was really the first thing I noticed.' Gilet dove into his dessert.

'Well, yes, Gilet, I had noticed that myself last night. But I don't see what that has to do with this murder investigation.'

'Only that she's much more appealing than her dead sister was, for what that's worth.' Gilet would not let his observation be discounted.

'Well, that's true, certainly, but what did she have to say about her dead sister?'

'She said it was ironic that on the night of her great honour her sister should get herself murdered. Said she was always wanting centre stage and that she had gotten it once again.'

'Did she seem bitter, angry, upset?' Corbet inquired.

'She seemed just sort of flat, kind of exhausted with it all. Said something about always being on the end of the tidal waves created by her sister.' Gilet finished his dessert.

'Did she elaborate?' Corbet was beginning to feel certain that he would have to talk to this woman himself and soon.

'Not really. Said that she had virtually brought up her sister's son and had been very good to her estranged husband, but now the son was dead and the estranged husband was involved with another woman, his son's former girlfriend.' Gilet waited for another question.

'Did she mention her friendship with Marie Marceau?'

'No, she didn't. Just said that she would be glad when this whole thing was over so that she could get on with her life. In fact, she had to cut our interview short because she was going to London to meet with her English translator and editor at Farber & Farber, I think she said. I saw no reason to detain her.'

'Did she comment at all on the death of the son, Raymond Lefèvre?' Corbet knew there was a lot that needed to be explored in this tangle of relationships.

'All she said was that her sister had abandoned him, that she had taken over his care and that he had died rather young. She seemed very fond of him. At that point, her time ran out, and she had to leave. Oh, yes, and she did say that Inspector Renard had made arrangements to interview her when she got back from London. That's about all.'

'What about her whereabouts and movements the night of the party?' Corbet couldn't believe that Gilet had failed to get this fundamental information.

'Oh, yes, that. Said she was at the party all night and had taken a taxi home at around 12.30 a.m. No one was with her. She just went home and went to bed. Says she found out about her sister when the police called her early the next morning.'

Corbet had begun to clear the dessert plates and take them into the kitchen. He brought out the silver coffee service and offered his guests coffee and an after dinner drink. They moved to the living room to enjoy this end to the meal.

'You can see already that Renard is going to be second guessing me all the way on this one.' Corbet glanced at his two assistants with some concern.

'Yes, Inspector, we can certainly see that he's trailing you, but we know you'll come through. We're with you.' Gilet tried to reassure Corbet of continued loyalty.

'I know you'll do your best, fellows, but I must confess that this is going to be a very trying process for me. I don't suppose Monique de La Tour told you where she was staying in London?' Corbet asked knowing it was more wishful thinking than probability that Gilet would answer yes.

'No, she didn't.' Gilet's expression said he saw the path Corbet's mind was taking. 'Maybe her friend, Marie, would know.'

'Yes, I'll call Marie and find out. I think I'll have to get to Monique de La Tour before Renard does. I want to see her in person and get a feel for her story myself. I hate to leave the Préfecture just now, but I think I can do it in two days. Of course, I'll fly. No time for ferries.'

Corbet was beginning to welcome the prospect of a little journey even on this kind of mission. It had been some time since he had been to London, and he had an old friend there he hadn't seen in quite a while.

'I'll book in at the Hyde Park Hotel for one night. You two will have to run things for me while I'm gone.' His assistants offered him their warm support in the form of reassuring smiles.

'Don't mention to Jouvet that I've gone.' Corbet wanted to try to do this little bit of research without tipping his hand to Jouvet who might in turn divulge the plan to Renard.

'I'll go first thing in the morning and be back before the next day shift at the Préfecture.' Corbet took the last long drink of his Armagnac and offered to refill the glasses of his guests who both declined saying they had to be up early the next morning. Inspector Corbet saw them to the door knowing that the Préfecture would be in good hands during his absence.

Chapter Twelve

With a call to Marie, Corbet learned that Monique de La Tour would be staying at the Russell Square Hotel in Bloomsbury. He had a vivid picture of the large bronze-coloured Victorian edifice that dominated a corner of Russell Square. Many years ago he had been a student in a summer programme of advanced courses in English Literature at the University of London. It was that summer that he had read the great Victorian authors – George Eliot, Dickens, and the Brontës – and then that he had met his old friend, Eileen Henley. He had lost touch with her in the past few years, but welcomed the opportunity to telephone her upon his arrival.

He phoned ahead to the Russell Square Hotel and managed to speak to Monique de La Tour before she left to meet with her English publishers. They agreed to meet for tea at four-thirty at Brown's Hotel, a British institution known to Corbet from his youth when he had visited London with his parents.

It had been awhile since he had spoken English, and he felt a bit rusty. However, his ability to read at a pretty high level had never left him. He had began to study English early in his educational career, and while he spoke with an accent, he had attained a rather advanced level of conversational ability.

As he rode into London in a large, square black cab, the city looked hauntingly familiar as though it had appeared in a dream he had had last night. The taxi let him out in front of the great, red-brick façade of the Hyde Park Hotel in Knightsbridge, a section of London convenient to everything. Harrods was just down the street from the hotel, and the Piccadilly line ran from there to Green Park where he would get off to go to Brown's later that afternoon.

Settling into his spacious, luxurious room, Inspector Corbet contemplated taking a bath in the magnificent English porcelain tub in his grand bathroom. He promised it to himself as a reward for work well done later that day. It was eleven a.m., and he had until four-thirty before he was to meet Monique de La Tour.

He telephoned Eileen Henley only to find out that her line had been disconnected some weeks earlier. In recent years her health had been failing. She must be, after all, eighty years old by now. When they had met during his summer of study, the thirty or so year age gap between them didn't seen to matter in the face of their shared love of literature. Eileen was very fond of Dickens and had taken him to see the Dickens House on Doughty Street in the neighbourhood of Russell Square. He had felt like a pilgrim going to worship at a shrine with a true believer.

Fearing the worst, Inspector Corbet called the Director of Studies for the University of London Summer School. Madame Lowney officially told him what he already knew, that Eileen was dead. She had died just before Christmas. She had been ill with cancer and had gone pretty quickly. The notes he had received in the past few years from her had been full of health concerns. In fact, she had taunted him that if he didn't come to London soon, she wouldn't be there. That was just before he had lost touch with her. Now here he was in London, and she was dead.

Chapter Thirteen

Wood pigeon, stewing venison, Barbary duck, stuffed quail. Counters of packaged stuffings of celery and walnut, apricot, sage and onion, plum and ginger, chestnut. Corbet was dizzy with it all. One could find anything at Harrods Food Halls. Cases of smoked fish, salmon, Atlantic halibut, scallops, salt cod, kippers. Dutch osso buco, Scotch beef, English lamb, Scotch oxtail. Gooseberry and lime and spiced plum cooking glazes for meats. Every kind of chutney – tomato, eggplant, plum. He wished he could have access to a kitchen to begin to experiment with this bounty.

Still stunned by the news about Eileen, he wandered around needing a focus. It really would help if he could cook something. He had never cooked a meal for her and wished he could roll back the clock. He decided to buy some packaged stuffings for experiments when he got home. Apricot and plum and ginger would go well with duck and game. He had never eaten tomato or eggplant chutney. And these new cooking glazes – spiced plum, gooseberry and lime – looked intriguing.

Purchases in tow, he sat down at the oyster bar among the panoply and ordered a dozen bluepoint oysters and a glass of Sauvignon Blanc. He raised the glass in memory of Eileen and wished her well in the next life. Since that next life was open to some question, it seemed all the more important to treasure this one, to make time for the things we love, to give of ourselves, to find meaning. He suddenly felt daunted by the reflection. He remembered how Eileen had struggled with a bad marriage, an unloving son, scars from the war. Maybe an effortless life was not worth living, but at times the struggle became downright Darwinian.

The thought of Renard scuttling around behind his back while he was away made him uneasy. How could one fight a battle on two fronts? The Americans had done it in World War II. Horrible as that war was, thoughts of the courage and determination shown by the British, Russians and Americans made him believe in miracles. He had often heard it said that that war was won with British brains, Russian blood and American brawn. An over-simplification, perhaps, but not untrue. This little island of Great Britain, led by its cherub warrior-statesman, Winston Churchill, had indeed been valiant against the German enemy.

Corbet loved Churchill and felt he could use a shot of his courage right now. He dropped his Harrods bundles at the hotel and headed for the Cabinet War Rooms, the underground bunker near Whitehall from which Churchill had conducted much of the war. This study in courage against overwhelming odds just might restore him.

Hurrying past Big Ben and down to Clive Steps at the end of King Charles Street, Corbet looked forward to seeing these rooms again. He had visited them years ago as a student. The Map Room, in particular, had impressed him then with its multitude of pinholes in the Atlantic Ocean.

'We shall fight on the seas and oceans. We shall fight with growing confidence and growing strength in the air. We shall defend our island whatever the cost may be. We shall fight on the beaches. We shall fight on the landing grounds. We shall fight in the fields and in the streets. We shall fight in the hills. We shall never surrender.' Churchill's voice boomed through the place as he entered.

When he came to the Transatlantic Telephone Room, he saw the famous scrambler which Churchill had used to confer with Roosevelt. Corbet shivered as he thought of how much Western Civilisation had depended on the alliance of those two men at that time. Perhaps there had never been a more important coincidence of men and moment. The bulldog courage of the cherub warrior along with his subtle genius as a master statesman made Churchill in Corbet's mind the real hero of the Second World War. It comforted him to imagine that he could find the strength he needed to fight his battles at the Préfecture and to solve the murder at hand.

Chapter Fourteen

Chapter I, The Follies of the Victors, 1919–1929. 'After the end of the World War of 1914 there was a deep conviction and almost universal hope that peace could easily have been gained by steadfastness in righteous convictions...' Thus began Churchill in the Penguin Edition of *The Second World War*. Corbet sat ensconced in chintz in a corner at Brown's waiting for Monique de La Tour who was now fifteen minutes late. He glanced around at the discrete, little groupings of people who were drinking tea and eating scones and cucumber sandwiches. His stomach growled. If she didn't arrive in five minutes, he would order a tea for two and help himself. He turned back to Churchill.

'I'm sorry I'm so late. They really are impossible. I'm not at all happy with the translator they've chosen.' Monique de La Tour sat down in the chair next to Corbet who put his book down and looked up at a stunning woman whose face of perfect small features was surrounded by a cap of short, honey-coloured hair and whose green eyes spoke of the sea. She was dressed in a chic, well-tailored, black suit. Corbet caught his breath and adjusted his position in his chair.

'Yes, I was wondering about ordering.' He cleared his throat. 'Too bad we're meeting again under these circumstances.' She was more beautiful close up than she had been at a distance at the soirée.

'Marie has told me so much about you, what a good friend you've been to her.' She lowered her eyelids and began to search in her purse for something. There was that word *friend*. Yes, he knew he was a good friend to Marie, but he did so want to be more than that. He hoped Monique would not sense that in his reaction.

'Yes,' was all he said. Monique drew a pack of cigarettes from her purse and put one in her mouth. Corbet felt a slight annoyance that he would have to endure another smoker, but it might be easier to tolerate from a beautiful woman. He took the matches from the table and lit her cigarette. She discretely exhaled to her left side away from Corbet. He began to relax about the cigarette.

'Marie has told me a lot about you, but I'll need to get the definitive version from you.'

'Of course.' She took another drag on her cigarette.

'Tell me about your relationship with Véronique. I gather it wasn't exactly a warm one?' Corbet waited.

'No, Inspector, it wasn't, but I think in recent years I had gotten over my active resentment of her and my anger about the way she treated her son, Raymond.' The waiter approached the table and took the order of tea for two. Corbet settled back into his chair.

'Actually, all I felt for her at the end was detached pity and occasional annoyance at her vain cruelty.'

'Vain cruelty, what do you mean by that?' Corbet waited.

'Well, she was about the most selfish, egocentric, cold-hearted person I've ever met or hope to meet. She delighted in other people's unhappiness, and the more so if it was caused by her. She abandoned poor Raymond when he was a little boy. For that I can never forgive her.' Her green eyes shone and colour came into her lovely cheeks.

'He was the creative genius in the family. He was able to develop his talent in spite of her.' Monique took a deep breath.

'Or maybe because of you?' The waiter placed the multi-level tray containing scones and sandwiches and pastry on the table and went to get the tea. Corbet helped himself to a cucumber sandwich.

'Well, yes, I guess you could say that. I really did raise him as though he were my own. Of course, I at least had the cooperation of his father, Georges. Véronique wasn't too pleased about that, but acceded to the practical reality that with me doing the parenting, she was free to lead her life of pedantic squalor.' She reached for a scone, some strawberry jam and clotted cream.

Corbet was working on the sandwiches, now enjoying one of smoked salmon. The tea arrived. Corbet poured Monique a cup, then poured his own and took a large sip. It was good, strong English tea, Brown's own variety, in fact. He had noticed that supplies of it could be bought at the counter in the lobby.

Being here was bringing back memories of his childhood visits to London with his parents. When his father's business was growing, and he was getting clients with international connections, they often came to London for long weekends during which his father would work, and he and his mother would sightsee. A visit to Brown's was always part of the programme. He was beginning to feel at home again in spite of the unpleasant nature of his mission.

'The woman I saw at the soirée the other night didn't look as though she were in good health. Do you know of any physical problems your sister was having before her death?' Corbet had finished with the sandwiches and now attacked the remaining scone.

'Well, she always drank heavily, but after Raymond's death, I think it got worse. Also she was taking tranquillisers. I know this not because I had ever discussed it with her, but because Georges told me. He had been having meetings with her about the divorce he wanted.' Monique reached for another cigarette. Corbet lit it.

'In fact, the night of the soirée Georges was supposed to pick me up, but he called at the last minute to say that he thought we should make separate appearances because Véronique might make trouble for him about it. What could I do but agree? I was almost late for my own party. I had to call a cab at the last minute.' She blew the smoke away from herself and Corbet and was silent for a moment.

'Oh, by the way, Inspector, speaking of the soirée, let me take this somewhat awkward time to tell you how delighted I was with the dinner you prepared for the occasion. Marie was right to praise you so highly for your culinary abilities. Many people have commented to me on the outstanding feast.' She smiled for the first time since they had begun talking, and her clear beauty shone the more brightly because of it.

'You're more than welcome, I'm sure. I had a wonderful time doing it.' He devoured the last bit of scone with jam and cream and looked around the room for the waiter. Now that he had begun, he felt as though he could eat at least one more scone. He ordered a separate order for two.

'I love to eat, as you can see. This afternoon tea takes the edge off.'

'Yes, it does.' She drank the rest of her tea. 'Inspector, I can't deny that I didn't like my sister at all, that I used to hate her bitterly, that there was definitely no love lost between us, but I didn't kill her, if that's what this is about.'

'It's really about these.' Inspector Corbet handed the handwritten Balzac quotations found at the scene to Monique. 'What were these quotations in your handwriting doing at the scene of your sister's murder?' The question had to be asked.

Monique examined the pieces of paper carefully. 'Why, these were notes I used in writing my book, *Balzac and the*

Creative Process. They must have been taken from my study at some point.' She seemed slightly flustered and shifted in her seat. She took out another cigarette. Corbet noticed that her hands shook as she brought the cigarette to her mouth. He lit it for her and waited.

'The one from *Le Lys dans la vallée* was found clutched in her hand. The other one was over on the other side of the room. It looks as if she were talking to someone about these quotations before she died.' Corbet noticed Monique shudder a bit and look again at the more crumpled paper.

'Inspector, I don't know how Véronique got these pieces of paper. I really don't.' She became more rigid and began to glance around her for the waiter. When he came over, she ordered another pot of tea.

'Well, if you don't know how they got into your sister's hands, what do you make of the content of the quotations?' Corbet poured himself another cup of tea.

Monique studied the more crumpled piece of paper. 'How weak and powerless is human justice. It only punishes open acts. Why does death and shame come to the murderer who kills with a blow…' She read the rest to herself.

'Sounds like a description of what Véronique did to Raymond, that kind of violence that is slow and subtle and worse than an aggressive, killing wound.' She looked at Corbet for a moment. 'Maybe whoever killed Véronique was trying to achieve some kind of Biblical justice, to punish her for hidden crimes she had committed.'

'That's certainly a perceptive reading of the quotation,' Corbet took a large swig of his now lukewarm tea, 'but why would someone want to implicate you in the murder by planting the quotations in your handwriting?'

'Oh, Inspector, I don't know. I can tell you that it was practically public knowledge that we were by no means close. Many people both in the academic and publishing worlds knew that.' Corbet had an uneasy feeling that there was something that Monique was hiding from him and that he wasn't going to get at it no matter how he chipped away. He persisted anyway.

'Maybe the other quotation can give us some more information.' Monique read it to herself. She stared into space for a moment.

'Well, this quotation, as you may know, was the basis for Dostoyevsky's *Crime and Punishment*. It comes from Balzac's *Père Goriot*.'

'Yes, I know,' was all he said.

'It's a bit puzzling, Inspector. Perhaps the person who killed Véronique felt he was going to get away with it and was thumbing his nose at exposure.' She leaned back in her chintz chair and sighed.

'Maybe whoever it was felt very smug about having implicated you with the handwritten quotations. They provided him or her with the same cloak of anonymity that the distance in time and space would provide the killer of the Mandarin.' Corbet shifted in his chair and looked at Monique. She now seemed a bit more relaxed, but he still felt there was much that she was withholding.

'It also suggests that many people would be tempted to kill Véronique if they felt they could get away with it. Only in her case, it would not be for an inheritance. It would be to rid the world of an evil force.'

'Some of the people to whom I've talked don't seem to believe that Raymond committed suicide. They think he had some help. How do you feel about that?' Corbet waited.

'Oh, that sounds like Georges. He's convinced that Raymond was murdered and that it may well have been Véronique who did it.' She reached for another cigarette. Corbet lit it.

'Another hidden crime to add to the pile.' Corbet was beginning to get a slight headache behind his eyes, his body's sign that he was becoming overloaded with information. The excavation required in this case would be slow and meticulous. 'Do you think that that could have happened?'

'Yes, Inspector, it could have happened. She was certainly capable of it, but I think she had carried out her violence in the early years and probably was letting it go at that. She seemed to be making some effort to mend fences with him, especially since he was becoming well-known in literary circles.' She crushed out her cigarette.

'You know, it's fairly common for men who go on to become famous literary figures to have suffered deprived and abandoned childhoods. Balzac was abandoned by his mother. Dickens was forced to suffer the vicissitudes of his father's misfortunes and went to work at an early age in a blacking factory.' Monique seemed restless and exhausted by the interview.

At the mention of Dickens, Corbet looked at his watch. The Dickens House was open late this evening.

'Yes, Dickens. I hope to visit his house on Doughty Street tonight before going back to Paris.' Corbet motioned for the waiter to bring the bill.

'Well, Madame de La Tour, I want to thank you for your time today. Sorry, I had to interfere with your visit to London.' Corbet paid the bill and began to gather his belongings to depart.

'Quite all right, Inspector. Even though I didn't like her, it's a very disturbing event, and I'll be glad when you've solved the crime.' She gave Corbet a soft smile that reminded him again of how attractive she was. Attractive and with a mind like a steel trap.

Chapter Fifteen

Corbet stood before a glass case containing manuscripts of and illustrations for Dickens's novels. He stared at the sketch of Oliver Twist asking for more soup at the orphanage. The scars of deprivation so intensely portrayed made him catch his breath.

He glanced around Dickens's study and wondered if it had ever been the scene of a murder or if it ever would be. The image of the body of Véronique Lefèvre at the Maison de Balzac reappeared. He imagined that he saw another body lying on the floor in front of Dickens's desk.

Coming back to reality, he was grateful for the warmth of the house and for the fact that at this late hour he was just about the only visitor. He completed his tour and went into the gift shop and bought a Penguin edition of *Oliver Twist*. It had been a number of years since he had read it. It was time for another look.

He nestled into the great, black cab for his journey back to the Hyde Park Hotel. What was it that Monique de La Tour was not telling him? Would it be something that she would tell Renard when he interviewed her? He felt his stomach twist at the thought of returning to the Préfecture. He would have a good dinner tonight to fortify himself for the journey tomorrow. Maybe he would take himself to Simpson's on the Strand, one of his father's favourite places to dine in London, for roast beef and Yorkshire pudding.

He glanced out the windows of the cab. Persistent streams of rain ran down them like tears that London shed for Eileen.

Chapter Sixteen

Early lunch was the best she could do. Blanche Ballard was a very busy woman she had informed Inspector Corbet, but she had agreed to meet him at eleven-thirty that morning at La Périgourdine, a brasserie at 2 Place St Michel across the river from the Préfecture. Corbet settled into a booth to wait for her. He didn't bother to look at the menu. He always had the onion soup and a green salad.

A dark, wiry, vixen-like woman stood at the front of the restaurant looking anxiously around. Corbet recognised her as someone he had seen at the soirée. He rose, approached her, introduced himself and led her back to the booth. Once seated in the booth, she rested her long, slender hands on the table. Her red, painted nails looked like talons, and her long, black hair, like her body, was wiry. The face that peered at Corbet from under that coiled hair was small, sharp and pointed, almost bird-like. Corbet supposed she might be attractive to some men, that she was a good match for Lefèvre's patent leather shoes.

'Madame Ballard, how well did you know Véronique Lefèvre?' Corbet ordered the onion soup and the green salad from the waiter and waited while Blanche Ballard ordered the same thing.

'Well, she was Raymond's mother, and you probably know that I was involved with Raymond Lefèvre?' She looked at Corbet quizzically.

'Yes, I've heard that from several people. Unfortunate that he died so young.' Corbet held her gaze.

'Unfortunate that he was murdered so young, you mean.' Her eyes glowed with a kind of dark energy that was mesmerising. Corbet looked away for a minute.

'Well, we'll get to that in a minute. I'm here to talk about the murder of his mother, Véronique Lefèvre. What do you know about that?'

'I know that unhappy women are the most vicious of creatures. I know that Véronique Lefèvre was an unhappy woman and that she tried to poison the lives of everyone around her. She abandoned Raymond at a young age and was only grudgingly accepting of his success as a writer, claiming association with him only after he had become noticed in her circles.' She paused to take a big spoonful from her steaming onion soup. Corbet did likewise. The onion soup was ever so slightly different in various restaurants, and Corbet enjoyed sampling the variety in a number of Paris establishments. This one was very docile and sweet and perhaps needed a little salt.

'You say she was unhappy. What exactly do you mean? She had become very famous for her critical articles and her biography of Beckett.' Corbet added the salt to his soup.

'Well, her forte was a type of acerbic criticism, as you know, sometimes verging on invective. Yes, she was bright and had some piercing insights. However, her opinions came not from a balanced, detached, reasoned observation, but rather from some twisted emotional lacuna in her psyche. Her vain narcissism demanded that she destroy anything she didn't understand, anything that threatened her. Even when she hit the mark, you couldn't trust it because the basis was infected with a bitter and hateful envy. She was very good at tearing down, finding holes or flaws, but she had no ability to exalt. I have my own theories about people like her.' She took a large drink of her wine and waited for Corbet to ask her another question.

'Such as?' Corbet waited.

'Well, Inspector, as a novelist myself, I'm rather leery in general about critics because almost every one of them is a frustrated creator. Since they are unable to create for whatever reason, be it lack of talent, lack of motivation, lack of discipline, whatever, they like to be always at the ready to spray poison and diminish the works of those who can create. It's just my theory. I've never met a critic who really didn't want to be a creator.' She glanced down at her long red nails and sighed.

'Do you know if Véronique Lefèvre ever wrote any fiction?' Corbet was scraping the bottom of his bowl of soup and eyeing Blanche intently.

'Well, as a matter of fact, after Raymond had published his novel, *Beyond the Night*, it was rumoured that she had begun to write a novel herself. More than the rumble of the rumour I've never heard nor had Raymond.' She began to fish in her bag for her cigarettes. Corbet leaned back in his chair and waited to do the honours.

'Needless to say, you didn't like her?' Corbet lit her cigarette and moved his head to the side to avoid the smoke.

'You could safely say that, Inspector. I didn't like her. She tried to ruin Raymond's life, and I think she murdered him.' Her eyes challenged Corbet.

'From what I understand, Georges Lefèvre agrees with you.' Corbet waited.

'Yes, he does. We both feel that Raymond was really healing from his spiritual crisis and was not a candidate for suicide. In addition, I'm almost positive that he never used drugs. They claim that he died of an amphetamine overdose. They never said what the drug was.' Blanche shifted her position in the booth and leaned her head to one side.

'An amphetamine overdose? Very interesting. And his mother, Véronique, was murdered with an overdose of digitoxin, not exactly an amphetamine, but a type of regulator for the heart.' Corbet finished the last of his soup and began to work on the green salad.

'She was taking enough drugs on her own to immobilise a small army.' Blanche sighed and took a large sip of her wine.

'Yes, she was definitely overdoing it with the barbiturates, but that wasn't what killed her. It was the strong dose of digitoxin that somebody put in her coffee.' Corbet watched while Blanche shifted in her seat.

'What do you know about these?' Corbet pulled out the Balzac quotations and handed them to Blanche who took them and began to examine them.

'These look like the subject of a quarrel I overheard between Véronique and Monique in Balzac's writing room just before I left the soirée that night. They were really going at it. It sounded to me as though Véronique was accusing Monique of having sent her those quotations as a veiled threat or something like that.' Blanche looked around for the waiter, and when he came, she ordered more wine.

So, this was what Monique was hiding, why she had become so rattled when he confronted her with the quotations. Corbet shifted in his seat and began to prepare to probe this new morsel delicately.

'What time was this that you overheard this quarrel?'

'Well, it must have been shortly before ten o'clock. I left the gathering at around ten. I was allowed to exit by the secret door that Balzac had used to escape his creditors. I had always wanted to do that.' She seemed very pleased with herself.

'Who let you out?' Corbet asked though he knew the answer.

'It was Jacques, the grounds keeper. Georges knows him quite well, and I persuaded him that he would be doing

Georges a favour if he let me go out that way.' Blanche began to work on her fresh glass of wine.

One of Georges's links to the Paris sewers, no doubt. Politics made interesting bedfellows. Corbet ordered a strong cup of coffee.

'What do you know about Monique's relationship with Raymond Lefèvre?'

'I know that she was more of a mother to him than Véronique was and that she had a lot of influence over him. Too much influence, as far as I was concerned.' She began to look around the restaurant as though anxious to leave.

'You didn't like her?' Corbet asked the obvious.

'Well, I didn't really dislike her. I just thought her approach to life a bit strange, especially when she tried to force it on Raymond.' Blanche began to tap her red nails on the table.

'What did she try to force on Raymond and how did she try to do it?' Corbet waited.

'Well, she has some strange notion about celibacy and its power to maximise a writer's creative potential. Apparently Balzac had had a similar notion, and she had adopted it. At any rate, she was less than pleased when Raymond left the priesthood and took up with me. I really think it was more a case of her not liking me than my not liking her. I believe she actively resented me.' Blanche ran her hand through her coiled hair and sighed.

'Was this idea of celibacy something that she thought good for herself as well as Raymond?' Corbet felt it would be a pity if someone as attractive as Monique de La Tour were hoarding her favours.

'Well, I don't actually know for a fact what she did with her love life. I do know that she has always carried a torch for Georges. I think the fact that he had been pressing Véronique for a divorce didn't set well with her.' Blanche reached for another cigarette.

'Yes, I suppose that as long as he remained good and estranged from her sister and she was mothering Raymond, she could feel herself part of the family somehow.' Corbet wondered how badly Monique might grow to want Véronique out of the way.

'About this quarrel, what else can you tell me about it?'

'Well, that's about it. As soon as I became aware of how heated the argument was, I left. I really didn't want to hear it.' For some reason, Corbet didn't believe this. He would have bet that she would have welcomed the opportunity to eavesdrop on such a quarrel between two women for whom she had little use.

'Why were you in such a hurry to leave? Ten o'clock seems awfully early to leave a party.' Corbet took a large sip of his now lukewarm coffee.

'Actually, Georges and I were supposed to have a rendezvous. I couldn't get him to leave with me, but he agreed to meet me soon afterwards at my place.' She smiled, and the corners of her mouth rose high enough to expose her rather unattractive teeth and unsavoury looking gums. Corbet looked away. She was better with her mouth closed.

'And did he?'

'Yes, soon after I left, he joined me at my place, and that was it.' She began to move the ashtray around on the table and fidget in her seat again.

'Well, Madame Ballard, you know that you will have to remain available for questioning as the investigation goes on?' Corbet gazed at her inquiringly.

'Yes, I suppose so. I'll be glad when this is over and we can get back to our lives. Véronique has always done nothing but make trouble for people.' She looked at Corbet with cold, dark eyes.

'So it seems,' was all he said.

Chapter Seventeen

The narrow steps up to Véronique Lefèvre's third-floor apartment on the rue St Jacques seemed to go on forever. Corbet reached the top, drew a deep breath and unlocked the door to Apartment Number 5. The crime scene crew had surveyed the place and was waiting for his final approval before beginning to process their collection of evidence.

The door opened onto a room full of the disarray of books, papers and cups. It exuded a stale odour of cigarette smoke, alcohol and something quite undefinable, but very unpleasant. It was as though something in the room had died a long time ago and been left to decompose. Corbet opened a window in spite of the January temperature outside. The fresh air felt good.

The crew had gathered groups of pill bottles and some letters on to a table for his inspection. He went back into the bedroom. The place felt haunted. The bed was unmade, the curtains drawn. Clothing was strewn everywhere, most of it in need of laundering or cleaning. It was hard to believe that someone could live at such a level of disorganisation.

On the bureau was a picture of a young man that was signed with the name, Raymond. He was a dark-haired, dark-eyed, very good-looking young man, a more refined version of Georges Lefèvre whose youthful picture was on the other side of the bureau. Corbet found it odd that she had kept his photo out in plain view.

He went again into the dining room and began to examine the pill bottles gathered on the table. There were many forms of barbiturates, sleeping pills, a thyroid medication, and a bottle of liquid digitoxin. Corbet picked it up. It was dated three years ago. Obviously, she hadn't been actively taking it now – but had someone borrowed it to get rid of her? And why had she been taking a cardiac medication in the first place?

He put the bottle in his pocket. He would personally take this to Ménager. At the end of the table under a small pile of papers having to do with her column at *Le Monde* and her publications Corbet found a group of letters bound together with a blue ribbon. The top ones were postmarked almost thirty years ago. He opened one and began to read it. It was a passionate love letter written in a bold, strong hand to Véronique from someone who signed with much love and the initial *R*.

A quick look at the rest of the letters indicated that they were all from the same person and that there were two letters at the bottom of the pile that were postmarked about three years ago. The first of these was a cold, unloving rejection letter, telling Véronique that in no way did he want her back in his life in spite of the existence of a child between them. It was signed *R* as was the last letter in the pile.

Corbet piled the letters back into the order in which he had found them and retied them with the blue ribbon. They were going to make interesting reading. He put them in his briefcase. He would go through them first himself.

The open window had cleaned out the air in the apartment a bit, and now a strong chill was settling over the place. Corbet closed the window, shivered and wrapped his coat tighter around him. He took one last glance at the haunting remains of Véronique Lefèvre's existence and headed for the door.

Chapter Eighteen

'Get your papers here, *Le Journal d'aujourd'hui*, read all about it! Sister's hair found at Lefèvre crime scene. Read all about it!' Corbet rounded the corner and headed towards the newspaper stand on Boulevard St Michel. How could they have obtained that information? Why were they printing it before even checking with him? It must have been leaked by Renard and his ghouls. He grabbed the paper, paid the man and headed for a seat in a café.

It seems that a subsequent search of the crime scene had turned up evidence of several strands of hair that they had now identified as that of Monique de La Tour, indicating that there may have been a struggle between the two women. No mention of who conducted the second search or why, just the Paris police. That despicable Renard. He will go to any lengths to undermine my credibility. The hot steaming cup of chocolate topped with whipped cream was little comfort as Corbet pored over the article and considered his next move.

Certainly now Jouvet would be on his back demanding that he take action, make an arrest even, before he would be ready to do anything of the kind. His instincts weren't telling him that Monique de La Tour was a killer. It was that simple. He would need to probe further before taking any action, this new evidence notwithstanding. He hoped he would be able to negotiate the room to do that. He considered ordering another hot chocolate but decided against it. He needed to get back to the Préfecture and talk to Gilet and Leroux.

Chapter Nineteen

A soft rain had begun to fall and was gently soaking Inspector Corbet's wool coat as he headed back to the Quai des Orfèvres. The Préfecture seemed like a large grey beast waiting in the fog and rain for him to enter and be swallowed up. He took a deep breath, quickened his step and felt his heart beating rapidly. He clutched tightly at his briefcase and kept checking to make sure that the rain water wasn't getting inside to damage the letters. No raincoat and no umbrella. What a time to be caught without them. The briefcase seemed to be holding its own better than his coat.

Once inside his office, he shed the wet, soggy coat, put the briefcase safely on a table, took a seat and reached into his drawer for a chocolate truffle. With the truffle in his mouth, he began to examine his desk for messages. Sure enough. A large note from Commissioner Jouvet. PLEASE COME TO SEE ME IMMEDIATELY. He swallowed hard and down went the truffle. He took a deep breath and headed to his sink to get a glass of water. Water in hand, he leaned back and gave his neck a good side to side stretch. He would need to go into Jouvet's office. There was no way around it. He noticed also that there was a message from Monique de La Tour who had obviously returned to Paris, and how he needed to talk to her. He wondered if Renard had spoken to her and if she knew how much trouble she was in.

Outside of the office of Commissioner Jouvet, he once again took a deep breath, knocked and was told to come in.

Jouvet was sitting behind his desk with his hands folded in front of him in waiting.

'Well, Corbet, you seem to be confirming my doubts about your ability to handle this case.' He licked his narrow lips and smiled exposing his jagged teeth.

Corbet took a seat in a small, wooden chair across from Jouvet. He would have to restrain himself when he felt like blasting his tormentor.

'Can you explain the failure of your men to find this very significant evidence, this hair that implicated the sister of the victim?' Jouvet waited.

'Well, Commissioner, I don't know when you sent another detail to the scene, but I do know that my men always check the scene twice, and if the hair had been there, they would have found it.' Corbet waited. He had to state what he felt to be the truth even if it served to antagonise Jouvet.

'Is it possible you sent your men between the two visits of my men?' That he had sent another detail at all was so insulting that Corbet was having trouble addressing it.

'As a matter of fact, Corbet, I believe, though I'm not positive, that the second detail didn't go to the scene until your men had finished. You remember I had suggested that you check with Renard as you went on this case? Didn't I tell you that I would be watching you very closely?' he inquired, licking his saw-like teeth.

'Professional courtesy might have suggested that you let me know if you were going to send other men to check the scene.'

'Corbet, I warned you. I told you I wasn't comfortable with your handling this case. You knew I was going to be right behind you. Why do you insist on acting surprised?' He kept his hands neatly folded on the desk in front of him.

'Are you positive that it's the hair of Monique de La Tour? Have you had time to do the definitive tests?' Corbet risked calling his bluff.

'We're almost certain just by colour and microscopic comparison.' Jouvet would not be daunted. 'We also have her admission to Renard that she and her sister had quarrelled that evening, and that Véronique Lefèvre had attacked her and pulled her hair in the fracas.' The ambush was complete.

Corbet sat silently contemplating this use of strong arm tactics. It was just like Renard to put a suspect's arm up the back rather than lay a more subtle trap, but he had obtained the admission from her and the information she had hidden from him. He felt a brief surge of anger at Monique for withholding this information from him and for making him a set-up for this surprise attack. He shrugged his great shoulders.

'Is that so?' He addressed himself again to Jouvet.

'Corbet, I can really understand your reluctance to get tough with this woman since she is Marie Marceau's friend.' He eyed Corbet slyly and waited.

'I assure you, Commissioner, that had nothing to do with it. I knew she was withholding something from me and that it would take me time to get at it.'

'But we don't have an infinite amount of time, Corbet. You know the kind of pressure I'm getting. You know the basics. It's imperative to move as rapidly as possible at the beginning of a case. You don't have time to take.' Corbet felt as though Jouvet were gnawing at his flesh. He showed no inclination to mercy.

'I would have gotten there, I assure you, Commissioner.'

'Yes, well, Corbet, I understand you did a little fast work in the form of a trip to London to interview Monique de La

Tour before Renard could get to her?' The jagged teeth looked covered with blood.

'Yes. I thought it important to get to her as soon as possible.' Corbet hated this awkward defensive position. He didn't play it well.

'Well, maybe it might be just as important to make an arrest as soon as possible since the evidence is piling up pretty rapidly against her.' Jouvet ran his tongue across his sharp teeth. He didn't even know about the quotations in Monique's handwriting found at the scene. Corbet determined that he would not learn it from him. He would have to negotiate his way out of the tight corner. He was silent for a minute while Jouvet waited.

'Well, Corbet, what are you going to do now? You know I could take the case out of your hands? I'd have every right to.' There seemed to be no end to his joy in tormenting.

'I can only ask you for a few more days, Commissioner. If I haven't made progress, say, by the beginning of next week, why I understand you'll do what you have to do.' This was as close as Corbet would come to begging for mercy or indulgence.

'Well, Corbet, what if during that time our prime suspect decides to flee? What do we do then?'

'I don't think that will happen, Commissioner.' He had to go out on a limb for Monique. 'I can put her under consensual surveillance.' He hoped she would go along with it.

'All right, Corbet. But you know that the circle is closing, and the clock is running. I won't entertain any more delay. If you can't make a strong case for not arresting Monique de La Tour by early next week, it will be a *fait accompli*. Do you understand?'

'I understand, Commissioner.' Corbet took his head out of the jaws of the beast.

Chapter Twenty

Corbet returned to his office and sat staring numbly at the piles of papers on his desk. With a sigh and a silent prayer, he began to go through the work that had piled up. He needed to try to gain some handle on a situation that was rapidly spinning out of his control. The glasses of mineral water and the chocolates he consumed while catching up on the paperwork helped to soothe him, and the sense of accomplishment from the rather mindless work with the forms on his desk made him feel somewhat more in charge again.

When he stepped out of his office to look down the hallway, he noticed that just about everyone had gone home for the day. He was glad for the silence and considered staying on an extra hour or two. His eye travelled down the long hallway to the end where he saw the light on in Renard's office. Better to talk to him when no one else was around. Corbet returned to his office, stretched his neck, took a long drink of mineral water and asked himself if he really wanted to confront him. The answer was he didn't want to. In fact, he wanted nothing to do with him ever again, but he knew he had to respond to the incursion into his territory by this ruthless rival.

He took a deep breath and headed for the door of Renard's office. He knocked gently, and the loud voice asked him to come in. Corbet entered and set foot into what was an unusually tastefully decorated office. There was an elegant oriental rug, and the furnishings were of a dark solid mahogany, objects obviously not provided by the Préfecture. It looked as though Renard had moved his home into his office. The man standing behind the large and imposing desk was tall, lean and wiry. His long, pointed nose made him resemble his namesake. He wasn't handsome, but there was something striking about him. He would be noticed in a room full of people.

'Staying late tonight, Corbet?' Renard moved his thin lips into a smile and motioned for Corbet to take a seat in the large chair in front of the desk. Seated, Corbet looked up into two coal-black eyes set a bit too closely together. Corbet shuddered at the glaring smile. He was beginning to feel like a trapped animal.

'Why are you so bound and determined to sabotage my efforts in this case? Do you really think undercutting me is the short and easy route to the promotion we're both after?' Corbet swallowed hard and waited while Renard folded his long body into the chair behind the desk.

'Now, Corbet, you know very well I had the permission of the Commissioner to double check your work. You surely know that, don't you?' He looked quizzically at Corbet.

'Unfortunately, I do know that, but that's still no excuse for this kind of unethical sabotage, for your leaking it to the newspapers, and you know it.'

'I may know it, but you also know that I don't care, and as for the newspapers, Corbet, the public has a right to know that the police are following each and every lead to solve this murder.' Renard rose to the challenge.

'Then I have no way to reach you, do I? I can't appeal to a sense of decency in someone who has none, now, can I?' Corbet glared at Renard, but knew he would have to retreat and be content with having made the effort even in the face of such resistance.

'No, you can't.' Renard got up and began to walk around the room with his hands behind his back. 'I think we're ready to make an arrest, Corbet, and I don't want you to sabotage that just because the suspect is someone you know. That's not very ethical, either, is it?' Renard stretched his lips into another grin.

'If that were really true, no, it isn't.' Corbet decided to roll over and play dead. He wouldn't tell him that Jouvet had given him a reprieve. There was no telling what he would do with that.

'Yes, Corbet, looks like Monique de La Tour is our murderer.' Renard's two coal-dark cinders burned into Corbet's face. As he rose to exit the torture chamber, Inspector Corbet's eye scanned the surface of Renard's desk and was caught by several pages of what looked like a report written in a bold longhand. He turned to exit but changed his mind and turned back to look at the papers.

'My updated report for the Commissioner, Corbet, if you must know.' Renard glared at him. Corbet turned on his heel and left.

Chapter Twenty-One

The Boulevard St Germain was throbbing with traffic and pedestrians all heading somewhere at lunchtime. The sun the day after the soaking rain felt warmer than it had in a while. Corbet quickened his pace. He had a luncheon date with Monique de La Tour for some very important conversation.

The Bistro d'à côté was almost empty. The waiter directed Corbet to a front seat near a window overlooking the Boulevard. He ordered a bottle of Chardonnay and settled in to wait for Monique. He didn't want to acknowledge the degree of his insecurity over the risk he was taking in trusting in her innocence. He would try not to let her see that.

Monique de La Tour arrived looking ashen and shaken, not at all the self-possessed woman he had met in London.

'I can't help you if you insist on withholding information from me.' Corbet began to examine the menu. They were featuring fresh tomatoes stuffed with a young goat cheese and a fricassée of salt cod with vegetables. These flavours, reminiscent of his youth in Provence, would provide some comfort.

'I know that now, Inspector. I'm sorry I didn't tell you all before, but I was terribly frightened. I think you can understand why.' Corbet could.

'But if you really are innocent, it's important that you do not withhold information that can be used against you by someone who wants to find you guilty.' The waiter took the orders. Monique followed Corbet's lead with the fricassée.

'We did quarrel that evening rather violently. It came as a shock to me. It had been years since there was such open hostility between us. Evidently someone had taken the quotations in my handwriting from my research and had sent them to Véronique. She was furious, and recognising the handwriting, immediately assumed I had done it and that I was trying in some way to threaten or taunt her. She accused me of the most awful things. When I denied any part in the matter, she physically attacked me. That's when she pulled my hair.'

'Do you know how someone got access to the quotations?' Corbet took his first bite of the tomatoes. It was the right choice.

'Well, now that you mention it, I did have a break-in at my apartment several weeks ago. I came home from a day of teaching to find my lock jammed and the apartment in disarray. However, at the time it didn't look to me as though they had taken anything. I thought maybe they were looking for money, and when they didn't find it only left the place in a mess. I keep what jewellery I have in a safe, and they couldn't get at it. I do remember wondering at the time why they had made such a search through my papers.' She drained her glass of Chardonnay.

'Do you have any idea why Véronique would have chosen the evening of the soirée to confront you with the quotations?' Corbet thought he knew the answer to that.

'Well, she never was a considerate person. Why not do it on the eve of my triumph? It was one more way to dominate and focus the attention on herself. Evidently, she couldn't help herself.' The waiter brought the fricassées steaming and fragrant to the table. Corbet savoured his first succulent bite.

'She accused me of lying in wait for Georges. She said it wasn't because of Blanche that she didn't want a divorce, but because of me, that I had already stolen her child, and that she didn't want me to take her husband, too.' Tears began to stream down Monique's cheeks. 'She nearly ruined what was going to be one of the best nights of my life.' She reached into her pocket for a handkerchief.

'I know this is difficult for you, but I must ask you if there is anything else you think I should know that you haven't told me.' Corbet waited.

'Well, Inspector, on the subject of quotations, actually, I must tell you that another Balzac quotation was found near Raymond's body. It was from *La Cousine Bette* and had to do with great men belonging to their works, with their tendency toward solitude, with the fact that they are incomprehensible to the majority of mankind composed as it is of dolts, the envious, the ignorant and the shallow. A rather harsh indictment of humanity that we took to be an expression of Raymond's despair rather than a comment by someone who had murdered him.' She now rummaged in her handbag for her cigarettes. Corbet did the honours.

'That, I assume, was not in your handwriting?' The fricassée was as good as anything his grandmother would have served him. He made a note to personally thank the chef.

'Of course not. It was typewritten. I don't know if they ever traced the source of the typewriting. I don't know what became of the note. There wasn't much of an investigation of Raymond's death. I think it was rather quickly classified as a suicide.' She was moving the pieces of cod and vegetables absently around on her plate. Even in her distress she was still amazingly attractive.

'I'm under some pressure from the Commissioner to get to the bottom of this case.'

'I know how this must look, Inspector. I'm sorry for the difficulty this is causing you, but I didn't kill my sister.' She crushed out her cigarette and took out another. Chain-smoking was a nightmare to Corbet who detested the halo of smoke that surrounded their table.

'Would you mind not doing that.' He surprised himself with the request.

'Of course. We smokers tend to forget how repugnant our habit is to those of you who aren't slaves to it.' She smiled her beautiful smile, and it took the edge off.

'Thank you.' Corbet began to contemplate dessert. He decided on some fresh pineapple.

'I seem to have lost my appetite.' Monique shoved her plate aside and ordered a strong cup of coffee instead of dessert.

'As a matter of fact, I have to ask that you agree to be put under a consensual surveillance to assure that you don't try to leave Paris. Otherwise, I'm afraid the pressure from the Commissioner to arrest you will be more than I can ward off.' He decided to lay it frankly in her lap.

'Of course, Inspector. I'll do whatever you want to co-operate.' Corbet believed her.

'My men will have a detail outside of your apartment night and day. It will also serve as a kind of protection for you.' Corbet was anxious that she should see a positive side to the surveillance.

'Very well. Thank you.' She stared into her coffee cup.

'There are some other things I must ask you about. I found some letters at your sister's apartment from someone who simply signed them *R*. They appear to be love letters, rather passionate love letters to Véronique from a man named *R*. Do you know who that might be?' The tart fresh pineapple was having a cleansing effect on his palate.

'No, I really don't know. She was always rather private about the actual specifics of her personal life. It was pretty well known that she was promiscuous, but beyond that, I don't know of anyone in particular with whom she was involved. You might inquire of Georges. I do know that they began to go their separate ways soon after their marriage. I wish I could be of more help.'

Corbet was trying to decide whether to go further with an inquiry as to her knowledge of Raymond's parentage. He decided to take the risk.

'From the letters, the last ones in the group, it appears that this *R* considered himself to be Raymond's father. What do you know about that?' Corbet waited while she seemed to absorb the shock.

'Why, Inspector, I know nothing about that. I always assumed that – and I'm quite certain correctly – that Georges was Raymond's father. I've never heard anything to the contrary.' She looked anxiously at her packet of cigarettes.

'All right. Now, I must ask you not to speak to anyone about our conversation. I can't emphasise this enough. Not anyone. Do you understand?' Corbet's earnestness was almost palpable.

'Yes, Inspector, I understand. My lips are sealed. I won't speak to a soul. You can rely on that.' Corbet felt he could.

Chapter Twenty-Two

Inspector Corbet rushed down the Boulevard St Germain to 1 bis rue des Carmes to the Museum of Historical Collections of the Paris Préfecture de Police. Gilet had verified that indeed Renard and his men had come to the Maison de Balzac between their sweeps for evidence. He had assured Corbet that his men, too, had found strands of hair at the scene and had collected samples from all suspects. They merely hadn't arrived at any positive identification of them by the time Renard and his men got there, made their cursory identification and then leaked it to the newspapers.

Corbet didn't hesitate to let Gilet see his displeasure at their lack of dispatch and to let him know what it had cost him. He instructed him to continue to check the hair samples from everyone who was a possible suspect. He felt pursued by some evil force. Perhaps with a visit to the museum, the history of past struggles and triumphs of the Préfecture might give him heart.

He entered the quarters of the police of the 5th Arrondissement, nodding as he did so to some of the officers who instantly recognised him, tipping their hats. Once on the second floor and in the museum, he began to look around at the various exhibits containing artefacts from the Ancien Régime to the present day.

He stopped in front of the section representing the life of the people of Paris in the nineteenth century. There was an exhibit documenting famous cases from that time, indicating that two infamous poisoners, a Monsieur Lafarge and a Dr Castaing, had been caught and punished. Indeed, there was a hair from the head of one of them taken after he had been guillotined. They had caught their murderers. He would catch his.

For a moment, he stopped before an exhibit representing the burning of the Paris Préfecture de Police during *la Semaine Sanglante*, the bloody week of 22–28 May, 1871. The institution of the Préfecture had undergone times of turmoil and trouble and had survived.

He had to talk to Georges Lefèvre again. There were many unanswered questions such as how he could have let the news about Renard's men's discovery get into the newspaper without even the slightest hesitation or effort to confirm it. Also, what did he know about the mysterious *R*? What about the parentage of Raymond? These significant details would go far in determining the direction of the investigation.

Corbet continued to wander a bit aimlessly in the museum as he plotted his next moves. First he would talk to Lefèvre and get some answers. Then he had some very disturbing questions for Ménager. He turned on his heel and exited the museum.

Chapter Twenty-Three

'You assured me that something like this wouldn't happen.' Corbet confronted a nervous and drawn-looking Georges Lefèvre who appeared to have been drinking rather heavily from a half-full decanter of Cognac on his desk. The room was blue with cigarette smoke. Corbet coughed a bit and looked eagerly towards the large windows.

'Do you think we could open one of those?' He waited while Lefèvre went over and opened the almost floor-to-ceiling window and let in some fresh air. Corbet took a deep breath and wondered whether he dared ask Lefèvre not to light up another cigarette. He decided against it.

'As I said, you assured me this wouldn't happen. Can you tell me why it did, why your newspaper leaked the less than definitive results of an evidence sweep by Renard's men?'

'Inspector, I'm trying to find that out myself. I was away for a couple of days, and all hell appears to have broken out here. When I gave you my word, I meant it. Apparently, there are some people here who didn't hear me very well. They are about to have their ears cleaned out.' He poured another full glass of Cognac and drank down a good portion of it. It looked as though he hadn't shaved for at least twenty-four hours.

'My people will have to interview those who were responsible for this, you know.' Corbet took a deep breath of the cool, fresh air that began to fill the room.

'Now, Inspector, is that really necessary? I assure you it won't happen again. You can count on that.' Lefèvre looked imploringly at Corbet.

'Yes, it is necessary. We have to find out just what happened, why this information got out before it was finally confirmed. It looks like a leak, and we need to know who in your operation was responsible for it as well as who was involved from the Préfecture. I'm sorry about that, but I'll need names.'

'Very well. I'll have Martin prepare a list, and you can take it with you.' He reached for the phone on his desk and dialled. With the receiver between his neck and shoulder he began to scrawl some names on a piece of paper from the desk. Martin entered, picked up the list and left quietly. Corbet noticed that Lefèvre's hands shook when he handed the paper to Martin. His silk suit and tie looked rather rumpled. If he hadn't slept in them, at least he hadn't changed his clothes for some time.

'Yes, Inspector, I went away on a little personal business, and all of this happened.' He reached for a cigarette. Corbet braced himself and leaned towards the window.

'Where did the trip take you?' He would take the bait.

'Actually, Blanche and I just went away for a couple of days. She had been after me for some time to do this, and I finally gave in. We were only gone, as I said, a couple of days.' Lefèvre began to pace back and forth the length of the room. Corbet followed him with his eyes.

To say that the man had lost whatever credibility he had had with Corbet was an understatement.

'Were you aware that your wife was seriously involved with a man named *R*?' Corbet watched carefully for Lefèvre's reaction to the question.

'My wife was involved with many men, Inspector. I'm sure I don't know the names of all of them and can't even remember the names of the ones I did know.' Only the tension in his facial muscles betrayed his discomfort. Corbet couldn't tell if he were merely being defensive or if he were out and out lying. This was often the case with those accustomed to dissimulation as he imagined that Lefèvre was.

'I found a group of letters dating back almost thirty years to your wife from a man who signed them *R*. Do you remember if early in your marriage your wife might have been involved with such a man?' Corbet would take it layer by layer.

'In no time at all after our marriage, Inspector, we began to go our separate ways. As I told you, it would be impossible for me to remember now. That doesn't ring a bell at all. Véronique was, at least for her, rather discreet about her extramarital activity as was I. So, I'm afraid I can't help you with that.' He took another large swig of Cognac. Corbet noted that just in the time he had been in his company Lefèvre had drunk enough Cognac to have rendered a less seasoned drinker such as himself inebriated beyond speech or comprehension.

Corbet swallowed hard and began to wish he had a glass of water. The fresh air was clearing some of the smoke, but it was still pretty hazy in the room. He needed to approach the question of Raymond's parentage.

'Do you suppose I might have a glass of water?' he inquired of Lefèvre who glanced over at a table containing bottles of liquor and an ice bucket. He got up from his seat and somewhat stumbled towards the table. Regaining his balance, he picked up a pitcher and looked deeply into it. 'I'm afraid we have none left. I'll have Martin bring some in, Inspector.'

The dutiful Martin entered the room in response to Lefèvre's phone call carrying a silver pitcher filled with cool water. Corbet eagerly took it from him, filled the glass and downed the contents in almost one gulp.

'The letters seem to indicate that this fellow *R* may well have been Raymond's father.' Corbet shot the javelin and waited. He noticed Lefèvre's already pale and sallow complexion become yet paler. He gasped before taking a swig of his comfort.

'Inspector, I assure you, I know nothing about this. I have had no reason to doubt that Raymond was my son.' His voice appeared to tremble a bit with these words. 'My God, hasn't my marriage suffered enough denigration? Do I need to learn this now?' He put his head in his hands and began to weep softly.

Corbet was not unmoved by this display of feeling, but he remained in his seat and waited. Lefèvre searched for a handkerchief and began to wipe his eyes.

'Believing that Raymond was my son gave me such comfort, in spite of my difficulties with Véronique. This just can't be, Inspector.' Corbet believed that Lefèvre really didn't know that *R* was Raymond's father.

'Well, Monsieur Lefèvre, the letters found in your wife's apartment would strongly indicate that. I'm sorry. I really am.' Corbet drained the glass of the last bit of water.

'On the subject of Raymond, when I was questioning Monique de La Tour about the possibility of Raymond's having committed suicide, she indicated that it was you who believed rather strongly that he had been murdered, but you didn't express that definitively when I spoke to you a couple of days ago. What are your real feelings about that, Monsieur Lefèvre?' Lefèvre looked rather surprised.

'Perhaps it's my exposure to Blanche, but, yes, I guess I've come to believe that he may well have met a bad end. I don't go as far as Blanche, however, in feeling that it was Véronique who killed him.' He gave Corbet a sidelong glance. 'In my more rational moments, I guess I still feel he may well not have had a strong enough motive to kill himself which is why I said what I did to you. It's hard to live in close company with someone and not begin to think like her.' Lefèvre let a long sigh escape from his lips and leaned forward in his chair.

Corbet rose from his chair, went to stand before the long window and began to take deep breaths of the fresh air. 'I'll have to get back to you again, you know,' he said with his back to Lefèvre.

'I know you will, Inspector.' Lefèvre's voice sounded very far away. Corbet let himself out.

Chapter Twenty-Four

Inspector Corbet sat reading *Le Monde* in the Taverne Henri IV on the Place du Pont-Neuf. A tall, lean, red-haired man headed toward him.

'Ah, Corbet, relaxing after a hard day's work?' Ménager eased his large frame into the seat across from Corbet and helped himself to a piece of toast spread with foie gras from the platter in front of him.

'Sauternes?' he inquired of Corbet.

'Yes, Jean-Pierre. I need something special today. It's good to see you.' Corbet took a bite of his toast spread with foie gras.

'Yes. I see your stomach has regained its equilibrium since our last encounter.' Ménager smiled his large-toothed grin and patted Corbet on the arm.

'It took me nearly all day to recover,' Corbet said somewhat hesitantly as he swallowed the last of his foie gras.

'But true Frenchman that you are, your gourmandise has triumphed, no?' Ménager grinned warmly at Corbet.

'Actually, this foie gras is quite good. The place is a little run down, but this is more than acceptable.' Corbet spread another piece of toast with the brown paste.

'But you didn't just invite me here to eat foie gras with you, Henri?' Ménager took a sip of the Sauternes.

'No, Jean-Pierre, I didn't. I want to discuss that bottle of digitoxin I sent over to you. As I told you, I found it in Véronique Lefèvre's apartment. I need to know the shelf life of that drug.' Corbet watched as Ménager took another large sip of Sauternes.

'That digitoxin had an expiration date of a year ago. So, it's unlikely that anyone would have been using it now.'

'How likely is it that it could have been used to kill Véronique Lefèvre?'

'Rather unlikely, but not impossible. Difficult to say. Have you had it analysed for fingerprints?'

'We could only find those of Véronique Lefèvre on the bottle. I suppose it's possible that she could have given herself that overdose. However, I think that's unlikely.' Corbet drained his glass and poured himself another. He ordered a fresh plate of foie gras. Maybe he just wouldn't eat a full meal tonight.

'All of her medical records and the autopsy I performed wouldn't point to her needing that drug. She didn't appear to have the kind of cardiac condition that would have called for it. Any idea what she was doing with it?' Ménager's tone became more serious.

'No, not really. It was made out in her name. That's all I know. I have no idea what she was doing with it, but I can speculate about what she might have done with it.' Corbet began to speak in a hushed tone. He was getting to the delicate part of the inquiry. He fortified himself with a large swig of the sweet, delicate wine.

'What's that?' Ménager waited.

'First I need to ask you some more technical questions, Jean-Pierre.'

'I'm all ears, Henri.' Ménager flashed his boyish grin.

'If someone were given an overdose of digitoxin three years ago and had died from it, if the body of that person were exhumed today, would there be any evidence of that overdose?' Corbet's brows moved together in contemplation.

'Well, after three years, all of the soft tissue would be gone, and it wouldn't lodge in the bones and hair as would other poisons. So, the short answer to your question is probably not. The drug acts on the soft tissue organs, the heart, the liver.' Corbet swallowed his last bite of the foie gras, which was beginning to lose its appeal. He decided to give the goose liver a rest, and he reached for the Sauternes.

'Just what is it you think she might have done with the digitoxin, Henri?' Ménager raised his bushy eyebrows in enquiry.

'I'm wondering whether she didn't poison her own son, Raymond. There are those close to her who feel certain that she did. He was supposed to have committed suicide from some sort of an amphetamine overdose. However, no autopsy was performed. He died three years ago. I thought that if we exhumed the body, maybe we could find out what happened.' Corbet pushed the plate of foie gras to the other side of the table. Ménager helped himself to a big piece.

'I don't think you'd find much to prove that kind of cause of death, Henri. However, if he were done away with by some other kind of poison, it might still be in the bones. It's your call.' Ménager's blue eyes twinkled.

'Well, on the strength of what you've told me, Jean-Pierre, for the moment, I think we'll let the dead sleep.' Corbet drained his glass and contemplated another, but decided instead to order a cup of coffee. The waiter removed the empty foie gras plate.

'They're really giving you a hard time, hey, Henri?' Ménager's eyes softened. 'I saw the papers. No doubt that someone is trying to sabotage your efforts.'

'Yes, Jean-Pierre, it's really a nightmare. It's one thing to have a difficult murder to solve and quite another to have those in your department trying to put every obstacle in your path as you try to do it. I don't believe I've ever really experienced such viciousness.' Corbet sighed and took a sip of the hot coffee.

'Well, Henri, you know you have the support of the inner circle – Gilet, Leroux, and myself. It's unfortunate that your promotion is looming so closely now. It doubles your vulnerability. However, rest assured that most people aren't fooled by Renard. He has his followers, those who are too afraid to do anything else, but that's not really a very secure power base, and you know it. Although, there's no doubt that it can raise hell with your serenity.' Ménager leaned back in his chair and stretched his long arms behind him.

'And how it has, Jean-Pierre. I thank you for your support.' Corbet began to gather his belongings to depart.

'Think nothing of it, Henri. You know I'll always be available when you need me.'

'Yes, and when this thing is all over, I want you and Isabelle to come over for dinner. It's my turn to entertain you. This is on me.' Corbet paid the bill.

'I'll look forward to that, Henri. Isabelle and I love sampling your culinary magic. You know, if all else fails, Henri, you could become a chef.' Corbet smiled weakly in the face of Ménager's wide grin.

'Right now that doesn't seem like a bad idea, Jean-Pierre. I'll think about it.'

Chapter Twenty-Five

Corbet started to cut through the Place Dauphine to head towards the Préfecture, but he changed his mind and decided to go over the Pont St Michel to Gibert Jeune. Browsing in a bookstore often helped quiet his agitation. He entered the front door, took the escalators up to the third floor and began to mount the old wooden steps to the fourth floor. It had always seemed odd to him that they had not put an escalator up to that floor, too, where all of the literature in paperback was housed.

He made his way to the bin containing the works of Honoré de Balzac. He took a Folio edition of *Illusions perdues* in his hand and began to peruse it. It had been some time since he had read this book about the entry of a young man from the provinces into Parisian society and the corrupt worlds of literature and journalism. He certainly felt as though he were reliving Lucien's disillusionment. He took the book to the cashier, paid for it and headed down the stairs all the way to the first floor. There were no down escalators in the building.

The crisp night air hit him as he crossed the bridge and headed towards the Préfecture. He hoped it would be late enough for most people to have left for the evening and he could have the place to himself. Maybe he would read a little before going home.

Upon entering his office, he noticed several messages and considered ignoring them until morning, but he thought better of it. The most curious and pressing was a message from Henriette stating that it was very important that he call her right away. He knew he couldn't ignore it.

Chapter Twenty-Six

Inspector Corbet inhaled the familiar Métro odour, a combination of burning wool and stale urine. He was headed towards Passy and the Maison de Balzac. He had promised Henriette that he would come over in the late morning to view the exhibition on Balzac and Printing and finish it off with a visit to her kitchen for lunch. She had seemed very agitated when he had spoken with her last night but had given him no clue about what she wished to discuss with him. She had only asked that he come and had insisted that she would prepare her special coq au vin for lunch.

Upon entering the door of the Maison de Balzac, Corbet's nostrils were treated to the deep, wine-laden aroma of the coq au vin which he could imagine simmering on the great black stove. He gave his coat to Michel who greeted him with a brisk 'Bonjour, Monsieur l'Inspecteur,' punctuated by the ever-present blast of alcohol.

The exhibition covered the first floor as well as some rooms down on the ground floor near Henriette's kitchen. Corbet began to stroll leisurely through the rooms on the first floor. He could almost feel the presence of the short, stout, mountainous Balzac. He saw him as he might have appeared when he had wandered these rooms, dressed in a white cashmere monk's robe with a gold chain, working frantically all night, drinking the beloved coffee that had eventually poisoned him.

There were many examples of books printed by Balzac at his print shop, including editions of La Fontaine and Molière. There was an example of the actual press itself, similar to the one described at length in *Illusions perdues*. Corbet had always found fascinating the process whereby a novelist used material from his own life to give birth to his creations. Clearly, much of the disillusionment of the young Lucien had also been that of the young Balzac whose venture into printing had left him defeated and horribly in debt.

In another cabinet in a small side room Corbet noticed a bill from a local merchant for sixty pairs of white gloves made out to Honoré de Balzac. No wonder he was always in debt. The idea of writing under the impending guillotine of debtors was for Corbet a rather chilling prospect. The intense anxiety he had felt over his own minor forays into indebtedness was not something he wanted to live with on a daily basis.

He descended the steep wooden stairs to see the rooms on the ground floor. As he did so, he was greeted with an even stronger scent of the coq au vin. His stomach gave an excited lurch. He was glad he had eaten lightly that morning. When he finished viewing the exhibition on that floor, he came through a room in the rear that led to the secret exit out the back door. He examined the door and the area behind the house. He shivered as he let himself back into the building and headed for Henriette's kitchen.

'Henri, I'm so glad you came. I really can't tell you how glad I am to see you.' Henriette rushed to greet him. He took her hands and held them for a moment. Her left eye was blackened, and she looked as though she hadn't slept in some time. He felt a slight pang of guilt over his anticipation of the coq au vin when she was so obviously in distress.

'Yes, Henriette, I'm glad to be here. The coq au vin smells heavenly, but you really shouldn't have gone to the trouble. I can see that you're very distressed about something. What happened to your eye?' He grabbed a ladder-back chair and sat down at the table which had been set in preparation for the luncheon.

'Oh, Henri, why don't we wait until we've had our meal?' She looked imploringly at Corbet.

'Well, Henriette, I'm not going to enjoy the meal very much if I know that you've been hurt, and there's something you're bursting to tell me. I'll enjoy it more if you tell me while we eat. All right?' He smiled at her.

'Very well, Henri. I'll dish it up, and we can begin.' She sighed and smiled a rather weak smile back.

'The exhibition is very well done. I imagine you've had many visitors?' Corbet placed his napkin on his lap and waited while Henriette brought him a steaming plate of coq au vin.

'Yes, we've been swamped with visitors from all over France, indeed from all over Europe. Since they only do these great exhibitions every three or four years, by the time they come around, everyone is really eager to come back for a visit.' She seated herself across from Corbet and arranged her napkin on her lap.

'Well, Henriette, what is it? What has you so upset?' Corbet took his first bite of the enticing coq au vin. The taste matched the smell. The succulent wine-soaked chicken, mushrooms, lardons and onions rested on a bed of homemade egg noodles. He took a piece of the chicken, a mushroom and a lardon and chased them with the noodles. As Henriette watched, a wan look of joy spread over her face.

'You've outdone yourself, Henriette.' Corbet took another bite of the divine offering.

'Thank you, Henri. It's my mother's recipe, and I think it's the best I've ever had.' She took her first bite.

'You must share it with me, Henriette.' It was certainly one of the best coq au vin he had ever had, too. 'But enough about the food. Please tell me what has happened. What has you so upset?' He took a large sip of the Côtes-du-Rhône that Henriette had poured for him.

'Well, you see, Henri, I found something that I think you should know about. I should say that Jacques found it the day after the murder of Véronique Lefèvre. He found it out back in the trash can at the rear of the house.' Her hands shook as she reached into her apron pocket and pulled out a bottle and a piece of paper and handed them to Corbet.

'Well, what have we here?' He examined the bottle. It was an empty bottle of digitoxin with a date of three months prior. The label indicated that it had come from a pharmacy in Lyon.

'It was wrapped in the paper.' Henriette looked anxiously at Corbet. He noted that the paper was a newspaper clipping about an art show at a gallery in Lyon featuring the work of a Margot Dutemps.

'He didn't want me to give it to you. He said we should just keep quiet about it, that we shouldn't get involved. I tried to ignore it, but it kept haunting me. I begged him to let you know he had found it. He refused. He said if I tried to contact you, he would leave me for good.' Tears began to stream down Henriette's cheeks. She reached into her apron pocket for a handkerchief and wiped her eyes.

'Go on, Henriette,' was all Corbet said.

'You see, Henri, I couldn't live with knowing that we had some evidence that might be very important to you and to the solution of the murder.' She blew her nose and sighed deeply.

'Yes, that doesn't surprise me, Henriette. Please continue.'

'Well, when I finally realised that no matter how I begged, Jacques was determined to conceal this piece of evidence, I decided I would take it and hide it where I knew he would never find it. As soon as he discovered that it was missing, he began to badger me about its whereabouts. I resisted him, even though he kept threatening to leave me. Eventually, he began to beat me. I told him I just couldn't be a party to hiding evidence in a murder case. He finally gave up, gave me a good beating and left.' She started to sob softly. Corbet reached for her hand.

'I don't mean to sound harsh, Henriette, but, frankly, you're probably better off without him.' Corbet surprised himself with his candour.

'That may well be true, Henri. He was always very difficult, but he had become much worse lately. He kept going out at all hours, would never tell me where he was going. Strange people would come to the back door, and he would let them into his tool shed. If I happened to be in the area, he would behave as though I didn't exist. When I questioned him about who these people were, he simply said it was none of my business what he did with his private life. It hasn't been easy.' She sighed deeply and dabbed at her eyes.

'Just how recently had all this been going on?' Corbet took a large bite of the coq au vin.

'Well, he's never been an easy man to live with, Henri. But I would say it actually began before the death of Véronique Lefèvre, and it has certainly accelerated since then. He would get as many as three or four calls a day from people I didn't know, and at least once a day someone would come to the back door. It was really getting on my nerves.' Her face looked more relaxed now that she had unburdened herself.

'What about Michel? Have you noticed anything unusual about his behaviour?' Corbet drained his glass.

'Well, now that you mention it, it was really strange. After the death of Véronique Lefèvre, Jacques seemed to drop his grudge against Michel. I would often come upon them talking upstairs, and they would stop as soon as they saw me. When I asked Jacques why he had changed his attitude, he gave his usual response, that it was none of my business.' She rose from her chair and began to gather the dishes.

'I have a wonderful cherry clafoutis for dessert, Henri.' The thought of the cherry-packed custard tarte gave Corbet's palate a thrill.

'That will be a perfect ending to an exquisite meal, Henriette.' Corbet helped her clear his place for the dessert.

'So, do you think it's possible Jacques had something to do with this murder?' Corbet asked the question that hung in the air as he took his first bite of the clafoutis. The sweet, dark cherries bathed in the custard were refreshing.

'Well, that's what I thought at first, Henri, and you can imagine how upset that made me. But I really don't think he would do something like that. He's pretty unscrupulous and even outright mean, but I don't think he would kill anyone.' Henriette's eyes pleaded gently with Corbet.

'Well, from what we know now, he wouldn't have had a direct motive to do it. If it were he, I believe he would have done it for the reward or to pay off a debt, something like that.' Corbet took another bite and eyed Henriette.

'Yes, Henri, that's possible, but I still don't think that's what happened. Believe me, I'm not trying to protect him.' She hadn't touched her dessert.

'Henriette, I know that. You're merely sharing your instinctive reading of the situation with me, and I appreciate it. Unfortunately, I don't know the man well enough to have a reading of my own. His behaviour does look suspicious, though, and I can't overlook it. I'll have to talk to him. Do you have any idea where I might find him?' Corbet finished his dessert.

'No, Henri, I don't. He left without telling me where he was going.' She rose to clear the plates and continue the never-ending process of keeping the kitchen clean.

'Well, perhaps I can speak with Michel. He might know.' Corbet rose and brought some dishes to the sink to help Henriette. 'Thank you so much for a wonderful meal, Henriette. I particularly appreciate it under these circumstances. I'll have to leave now. I've got a lot of digging to do before I'll be finished with this case.' Corbet retrieved his coat and gloves from the coat rack.

'Henri, I'm glad you could make it. I'm sorry I had to give you more upsetting news, but maybe it will help you solve the murder.' She smiled a weak smile and walked Corbet to the door.

'You've done the right thing, Henriette. And, don't worry, it will all work out in the end. I know it will.' He took her hands for a moment, gave her a kiss on the cheek and headed up the stairs.

At the guard's station on the first floor, he looked around for Michel. The woman on duty said that he had left for the day and that she had no idea where he might have gone.

Chapter Twenty-Seven

The dark, blustery sky above the Place St Michel threatened rain. Corbet hurried across the bridge to the Préfecture. As he approached his office, he found Gilet outside waiting for him.

'Inspector, I'm glad you're back. I need to see you.' Gilet followed Corbet into his office without invitation.

'Well, give me a minute to get my coat off, Gilet.' Corbet was digesting not only the coq au vin, but also the new twist in the case presented by Henriette's revelations.

'Sorry, Inspector.' Gilet waited.

'Go ahead. What's up?' Corbet went to the small refrigerator and took out a bottle of mineral water, opened the lid and poured himself a glass. 'Would you like some?' he asked Gilet.

'No, thanks, Inspector. I've followed up on Lefèvre's story. Talked to several people over at *Le journal d'aujourd'hui*. They say he wasn't away for two days, only one afternoon. They all insist that they take their orders from him and that that business about the hair appeared in the paper because he authorised it.' Gilet was pacing in front of Corbet's desk.

'Is that so? Well, he has now not only broken a promise to me, but he has also outright lied. Did he really think I wouldn't find this out?'

'I don't know, Inspector. But that's what the people at the paper told me.'

'Well, Gilet, I'll have to get to him a bit later. I've just received some very interesting information and evidence from Henriette over at the Maison de Balzac.' He handed the bottle of digitoxin to Gilet.

'That was found just outside of the Maison de Balzac the day after the murder, found by Jacques, Henriette's husband, who has now taken off for parts unknown. I want you to track him down. I also want you to get hold of the doorman, Michel, the one I've told you is always slightly inebriated.' Corbet finished his water.

'Yes, Inspector, I'll do what I can.'

'Just find out their whereabouts. Have Leroux keep an eye on them until I can talk to them. I'll get back to Lefèvre myself. In the meantime, I'm going to go down to Lyon and check out the identity of this Margot Dutemps. I'll be gone for the day tomorrow. I'll leave you in charge. Do you think you can handle it?'

'Yes, Inspector, I think I can.' Gilet beamed.

'Put Lefèvre under surveillance, but don't let anyone speak to him until I get back.' Corbet popped one of his chocolates into his mouth.

'Will do, Inspector.'

Chapter Twenty-Eight

Corbet rushed past the Hotel de Ville towards Marie's apartment. The rain that had only threatened the day before poured down with a vengeance. He was prepared with his raincoat and large umbrella. He sloshed his way through the two short blocks to her apartment building.

Marie greeted him at the door with a very warm hug. She had been becoming progressively more affectionate, and he was beginning to dare to hope that the tide was turning in their relationship. He followed her up the narrow stairs to the apartment. She excused herself and went into the bedroom to finish her make-up. She had jumped at the chance to take the TGV with him to Lyon while he investigated the evidence he had gotten from Henriette.

He sat down on her comfortable, overstuffed sofa and glanced at the two walls covered with leather-bound editions of Balzac, Stendhal and Zola. He remembered how she loved to say that these authors were her best friends. One of the walls contained large, coloured lithographs of country scenes done by Gantner, a twentieth century French artist whose work Marie admired.

He glanced up at the beams that ran across the ceiling. She had proudly informed him that those were the same beams that had been there at the time of Racine and Corneille. She had bought the antique apartment and had lived in it since her divorce about fifteen years ago.

The leather-bound volumes of Proust's *À la recherche du temps perdu* on the end table caught his eye. He felt a slight chill as he thought of Roger Albert, the Proustian scholar who had lived in the apartment with Marie before he was murdered. He quickly tried to erase that image and focus on the present.

Marie came out of the bedroom. She offered him a drink which he declined, saying that they had better get going lest they miss the train.

She made her way over to the sofa where he sat and, without saying a word, took his hands and pulled him up towards her. Corbet was a bit stunned but delighted. She put her arms around him and gave him a tender kiss on the mouth. It caught him off guard. He may have hoped for this, but he certainly hadn't expected it. He reached his arms around her waist and held her close to him. His dream was coming true. They stood like that for some time before Marie spoke.

'I know you're having a very difficult time with this case, Henri. I want you to know that someone cares.' She smiled at him and he held her tighter.

'Thank you, Marie. That means the world to me. You know it does.' He buried his face in her neck for a moment.

'All right. Let's be off.' Marie moved away rather quickly as though she had suddenly become aware of what she was doing. 'We can't miss that train.'

Corbet followed her down the stairs.

Chapter Twenty-Nine

'Now you see why I wanted you to come with me.' Corbet beamed across the table at Marie. The crowd at the Café des Fédérations was just beginning to thin from the early luncheon rush. It was an old-fashioned Lyonnais bistro with rustic furnishings and decor.

'Yes, Henri, I've heard about their rabbit with mustard sauce.' Marie smiled warmly at him. Her eyes seemed to acknowledge the new level of intimacy between them.

'Best I've ever had.' Corbet was examining the menu carefully to see whether it had changed since the last time he had eaten there. It hadn't.

'Well, then we needn't equivocate, hey, Henri?' Marie closed her menu. They both ordered the rabbit with mustard sauce which would come accompanied by buttered noodles and a bottle of Beaujolais-Villages.

'What did you find out, Henri?' Marie took a sip of the wine Corbet had poured for her.

'I got the address of Margot Dutemps from the phone book, but when I went to check it out, her neighbour told me she was away for the day visiting some relatives in the country and wouldn't be back until tomorrow.' Corbet sighed and took a sip of wine.

'It seems that Margot Dutemps is a seventy-five year old woman who lives alone. She has had a heart condition for about seven years and needs the digitoxin to regulate her heart rate. That was all I could learn from the neighbour.

That means I'll have to stay down here to check things out tomorrow.' Corbet eyed Marie enquiringly.

'That's fine, Henri, I can take the TGV back by myself tonight. I really don't mind.' Corbet had the answer to his silent question. Marie wasn't ready to be spending the night with him.

'You know, Henri, it's really amazing to think that we can get down here from Paris in two hours on the train. No wonder late lunching in Lyon has become so popular with those who know what's in.'

'Yes, Marie, though I'm not sure I know what's in, as you say.' He smiled back. 'I'm afraid it's only Madame Dubois's good cooking that motivates me.' The waiter brought the steaming plates of rabbit to the table. Corbet adjusted his napkin and prepared to feast. He waited with some difficulty until Marie had taken her first bite.

'Oh, Henri, how divine this is!' Corbet took his first bite of the tender rabbit bathed in the tart mustard sauce cushioned with large quantities of chopped onions and fresh herbs. His palate began to sing with the joyous flavours. It certainly was as good as the last time he had eaten it here.

'Yes, I thought you might like it.' Corbet noticed that Marie had begun to look even more beautiful. More of the tension had vanished from her face, and she was radiant. His heart gave a little leap as he dared to let himself hope of joys to come.

'Indeed I do, Henri. Thank you. But enough of me. This case has become quite troublesome to you, hasn't it?' She put her fork down and waited.

'It certainly is one of the more difficult I've had, especially with the backdrop of the current politics of the Préfecture.' He took a large sip of wine.

'Fighting sabotage can't be easy.' Marie looked tender and sympathetic. Corbet was almost glad for all the turmoil over the case if it had earned him that look.

'It's not. I must tell you that I've agreed to a deadline with Jouvet. If I can't come up with a strong lead to an arrest by the beginning of the week, he'll have to arrest Monique.' Corbet wished he had been better able to cushion the blow.

'Oh, no, Henri.' Her eyes pleaded with him. 'I don't think in my wildest imagination that Monique could kill anyone.' Marie's eyes began to fill with tears.

'I don't think so, either, Marie, but he has the evidence of her hair found at the scene, the fact that she quarrelled with Véronique earlier that evening, the long-standing animosity between them. It all points to her involvement in the murder, I'm afraid, or at least enough so that Jouvet can listen to the urging of Renard in the matter.' Corbet wrapped the last bit of rabbit up with some noodles and popped it into his mouth. He was sorry that his plate was empty and considered ordering another portion, but he thought better of it. He remembered the raspberry tarte he had seen on the menu, and that would be a fine way to finish the meal.

'I've been thinking a lot about the means of murder, the use of the digitoxin. Often means will give a clue to motive if you look carefully enough.' The waiter brought the gleaming red tarte to the table. Corbet took his first tart-sweet bite.

'Well, Henri, first of all, it has to do with altering the heart rate. Coffee alters the heart rate, too. Balzac used to drink large quantities of coffee, as you know. He had his own special blend of three or four different types to assure a good strength.' Marie watched as Corbet devoured the tarte.

'Yes, he certainly did use coffee as a drug, Marie. There's no doubt about that. It was an aid to his creativity, and it also killed him by constantly over-stimulating his heart. Certainly, that's what digitoxin does, also, in a high dose. And it was put in coffee, too.' Corbet's furrowed his brow.

'Henri, since we're eating rabbit with mustard, I must tell you that I've also heard that Balzac used to have a pot of mustard near his writing table and would often inhale it as a stimulant.' Marie smiled warmly at Corbet.

'Yes, now that you mention it, I've heard that, too. I guess he needed whatever he could get to keep writing those long hours. But why would our murderer choose to use digitoxin in coffee? Is there a message in that? That's what I need to know.' Corbet took a long drink of the strong, hot coffee.

'Was the murderer trying to make some statement about drug-induced creativity and the dangers of it? Is that what you mean, Henri?'

'Well, something like that, Marie. I hate to say it, but the fact that Monique was involved in writing on Balzac and creativity does seem to fit in here, too.' He lowered his eyes.

'What statement could Monique have been making by using digitoxin to kill her sister, Véronique?' Marie looked puzzled.

'Maybe that she was able to get only the destructive effects of a drug used for creativity. It would appear that Balzac got the positive and the negative effects from his use of coffee. As we know, Véronique was drugging herself pretty heavily with barbiturates and other things. Maybe the murderer was just helping her finish the job?' Corbet waited.

'In some way it certainly was a comment on her creativity. I can see that, Henri, but I don't like the easy path that makes to Monique.' Marie frowned.

'Maybe that's just what the murderer wanted, to suggest a strong link to Monique, with the evidence of the hair, the quarrel, and even the choice of digitoxin. Very interesting, indeed.' Corbet seemed to get lost in his own thoughts.

'It would have to have been someone who knew Monique pretty well.' Marie's eyes reflected the hope she was beginning to feel.

'That might really narrow the field. What do you make of these?' Corbet pulled the Balzac quotations found at the murder scene from his pocket and handed them to Marie who took a few minutes to examine them carefully.

'They're in Monique's handwriting. Henri, do you mean to tell me these were found in Balzac's writing room where Véronique was murdered?' Her eyes showed her incredulity and confusion.

'Yes, I'm afraid so, Marie.'

'Well, the one about the Mandarin was the one that inspired *Crime and Punishment*. I'm sure you know that, Henri?'

'Yes, I know that, Marie, but what do you think it says about our murderer?'

'Something about anonymity, at least. That the murderer was going to commit this murder because the opportunity was too ripe to resist.' Marie finished the last bite of the raspberry tarte.

'Yes, that certainly makes sense. Sort of, you would do this, too, if you knew you could get away with it. I'll get away with it, so why not.' Corbet ordered another cup of coffee.

'But what about the other one, the one about the invisible crime, Henri?'

'Well, that's very interesting, Marie. It indicts a person who kills with a slow form of torturous poison. That could be psychological abuse and neglect, I would say.'

'Such as that of Véronique towards Raymond, her son?' Marie sighed deeply.

'My thoughts exactly, Marie. The murderer is commenting on Véronique's abuse of Raymond, there's no doubt in my mind about that. But why?' Corbet took the last swig of his coffee.

'Why, indeed?' Marie fell silent.

'I don't have to underline that this could also strongly point to Monique.' Corbet looked directly at Marie.

'No, Henri, you needn't. It's all too clear. My God, how much trouble one human being can make for another when he sets about to do it. Who would want to incriminate Monique, to do her this kind of damage?'

'I have some people in mind, Marie, but nothing really fits yet. I need to do more digging. Thanks so much for your help and for coming down here with me today. It's meant a lot to me.' He took her hand and held it while the waiter cleared the table and brought the bill.

Chapter Thirty

Corbet hurried down the rue du Boeuf in Le Vieux Lyon towards the apartment of Margot Dutemps. It was in an antique section of the city which had recently been renovated and was now inhabited by antique dealers and artists.

The door of Madame Dutemps's apartment opened before he could finish knocking. It was situated on the second floor of an old, five-story building. Corbet's nostrils were hit with a strong odour, a mélange of clay, stale cooking and old skin.

The face of the woman who greeted him was drawn and very wrinkled, giving her the appearance of someone much older than her seventy-five years. Her frail, slim frame carried almost no flesh. As she moved into the apartment and offered to take Corbet's coat, she reminded him of a bent, old broomstick. She had wild, curly, greyish-white hair which she had tried to pull back at the nape of her neck but which kept escaping in little strands all over her head.

The living room was shabby with old, but once very fine, furniture. Just behind that was a smaller room from which emanated a very pronounced smell of clay. It was her studio. She was a sculptor.

'Do sit down, Inspector,' she invited Corbet to sit on a worn tapestry-covered sofa. 'Sorry I wasn't here when you called yesterday. What can I do for you?'

'Well, Madame Dutemps, this was found at the scene of the murder of Véronique Lefèvre which occurred in Paris a few days ago at the Maison de Balzac.' He handed the empty digitoxin bottle and the newspaper clipping to her.

'My God, I wondered where that had gone. It's been missing. I even had to get a new prescription before the time was up on this one.' She brushed some of her tangled hair out of her face. Corbet couldn't seem to get used to the cacophony of smells. The most disturbing was the odour of old flesh. He kept resisting a strong impulse to just leave the apartment.

'Do you have any idea how this bottle could have gotten to the Maison de Balzac in Paris, Madame Dutemps?' Corbet held his breath to minimise the number of times he would have to breathe in that odour.

'Not in the least, Inspector. I know a few people in Paris, but I'm sure they wouldn't have stolen my medicine. I mean, why would they, you know?' She got up and circled the room like a bent-over bird.

'Well, you'll have to tell me who they are, give me a list. I'll need to talk to them.'

'Well, Inspector, they're art dealers. But, just a moment, while I get some paper.' She went to an old desk and took out a sheet of yellowed paper and began to scribble some names on it. When she had finished, she handed it to Corbet.

'These are all I can think of now.' Corbet took the paper and noticed the names of three art dealers.

'Do they ever visit you here in Lyon?' Corbet's eye kept being drawn into the studio.

'No. I always take my work up to Paris to sell it. They can't be bothered coming down here. Of course, the ones I've been dealing with a long time know my work and will often commission things to be done ahead of time. But, no, I do the delivering.'

'Madame Dutemps, would you mind showing me some of your pieces?' Corbet needed to get into that studio.

'Why, of course, Inspector. I'm flattered that you asked.' She led Corbet into the small studio behind the living room. In it was a long table covered with many pieces of sculpture in all stages of completion. Like many artists, her work seemed to have a trademark appearance. She preferred to do busts, and the heads, necks and shoulders were slightly more elongated than they might have been in real life, something like the works of Modigliani.

'Very impressive, Madame,' was all Corbet said. He studied the busts of a man and a woman carefully, trying to see if he could determine the identity of the models. He couldn't, and indeed he wondered whether it wouldn't be difficult in any case with her particular affinity for elongation.

He couldn't shake the feeling that there was much that Madame Dutemps was withholding from him any more than he could shake the smell of stale flesh. How to pry her open was a problem, and he feared that he wouldn't like what he uncovered when he did.

'Yes, I'm kept pretty busy, even at my age and with my bad health.' She bent herself through the door and headed back into the living room.

'Madame Dutemps, are you sure you've included everyone you know in Paris on this list?' Corbet pressed.

'Yes, Inspector, I am.' She closed her shell even tighter.

'Are you telling me that you don't know Georges Lefèvre, Monique de La Tour or Blanche Ballard? Those are some of the people closest to the murder victim, Véronique Lefèvre.'

'Well, Inspector, I won't deny that I've heard of Véronique Lefèvre. She was a famous critic and writer for *Le Monde*. Of course, I knew her by reputation, and I knew of her murder. But I don't know those other people, not at all. I'm afraid I can't help you.' Or you won't, thought Corbet.

'Now, Madame Dutemps, I need to ask you about your whereabouts on Saturday evening, a week ago, the night that Véronique Lefèvre was murdered. Where were you?'

'Why, I believe I was here at home, Inspector. I live alone, you know, so there's no one who can tell you that I'm telling the truth.' Her face twisted into a wrinkled frown.

'What about the neighbour I spoke to yesterday? Would she be able to corroborate your story?' The smell was becoming suffocating.

'I don't think so, Inspector. You see, she usually leaves on weekends to visit her son in the country. It was unusual that she was around this weekend. So, the answer to your question is no. You can check with her if you want to.'

'Very well, Madame, I will. Thank you. I'll be back to you when I've talked with these dealers. I'll let myself out.' He held his breath and made a quick exit.

Chapter Thirty-One

Once back in Paris, Corbet went right into Notre-Dame. The high mass was half over, but he entered anyway because he needed a respite. He took a seat fairly close to the altar. There was the usual crowd of Parisians and tourists from all over the world who wandered in and out of Notre-Dame each day, even during a high mass celebration.

Inspector Corbet settled into his small, wooden chair and let the chants take his spirit. He was feeling very fatigued, frustrated and haunted by his encounter with Margot Dutemps. There was something familiar about her, but he couldn't place it. It was as though he had met her somewhere before or someone quite like her. Racking his brain was producing no clues. He decided to try to let it go.

The priests in their white and multi-coloured vestments came down the aisle shaking incense and chanting. Corbet inhaled the smoky, spicy odour of the burning offering. It was an antidote to the assault his nostrils had taken at Margot Dutemps's apartment.

The priests began to divide up and go to separate parts of the congregation carrying their chalices full of Holy Communion. Corbet found himself automatically getting into line to receive it. Even though he was not a practising Catholic, he was often inspired to participate in the ritual of the church. He took the wafer from the young priest who informed him that it was the body of Christ. He put it in his mouth. The dry, dusty taste was familiar and comforting.

Corbet knelt down, bent his head and leaned it on his folded hands in a kind of prayer. It was perhaps only a miracle that could help him now. The clock was ticking. There had been a note from Jouvet to report to him first thing in the morning. Corbet shuddered at the thought of the kind of pressure he was certain Jouvet was going to bring to bear on him to arrest Monique for the murder of her sister. He was going to have to move very fast and have a windfall of luck to beat that clock. He silently asked the help of the Almighty.

As the crowd filed out of the large old cathedral, Corbet was swept along with them feeling calmer and more hopeful. The library at the Centre Pompidou would be open on Sunday afternoon, and he needed to get hold of three years of back issues of *Le Monde*. It would probably take him the afternoon to do that unless he found what he was looking for right away, but first he needed to touch base with Gilet at the Préfecture.

Chapter Thirty-Two

'That's what he says, Inspector.' Gilet was pacing around Corbet's small office. 'Says he won't tell us who it was unless we promise that we won't bring charges against him for withholding evidence.' Gilet ran his hand through his thick hair and looked Corbet in the eye.

'Well, did he say what time Michel let the person in and what time he or she left?' Corbet was looking in his drawer for a chocolate.

'Says it was late, around twelve-thirty or so. Many people had already left the soirée by then.'

'I'll have to speak with him later. But now I must do some research at the library. Continue to hold him, and whatever you do, don't let him get in touch with Henriette. I don't want him causing her any more trouble.' Jacques had been picked up for causing a disturbance in a local café the night before.

'Will do, Inspector. He won't go anywhere.' Gilet stopped in front of Corbet's desk and folded his hands behind his back.

'Any luck with Michel?' Corbet got up to get some mineral water from his refrigerator.

'No, Inspector, we can't seem to locate him. Nobody at the Maison de Balzac seems to know where he went. He just disappeared. But they tell me that he often does that. Goes sometimes for days, but he always turns up.'

'Well, we had better find him soon. Keep on it.'

'Will do, Inspector.'

'And Lefèvre?'

'We've got him under surveillance. He's spending a lot of time at the newspaper. Doesn't seem to be going home. But we're watching him very carefully.' Gilet smiled his broad smile and began to pace again.

'Margot Dutemps, the woman whose prescription bottle was found at the scene by Henriette, says she has no idea how the bottle got there. Says she doesn't know anyone in Paris except some art dealers. Here's a list of them. I want you to check them out, ask them what they know about her, about her contacts in Paris.' Corbet ate another chocolate.

'I'll get on this first thing in the morning, Inspector. We're also checking on some hair samples that were found at the scene along with those of Véronique Lefèvre and Monique de La Tour.'

'Well, keep at it. I know I'm going to get pressure from Jouvet in the morning, and I want to be ready for him.' Corbet leaned back in his chair and drained his glass of mineral water.

Chapter Thirty-Three

'Well, Corbet, you must know your time is up now?' Jouvet grinned exposing the saw in his mouth.

'Yes, Commissioner, I know the clock is running.' Corbet swallowed with difficulty and shifted his weight from one foot to another. He hated having to ask anything of such a predator, but he must. How to do it without giving him access to information that he could use against him was the trick.

'My men are still working on some hair samples they found at the scene. I'll need at least another day on that.' Corbet held his breath.

'Another day? I told you before that if you couldn't show me a strong line to an arrest by today, we were going to arrest Monique de La Tour, and I meant it, Corbet.' Jouvet's outstretched and folded hands belied the urgent anger of his delivery.

'Yes, Commissioner, I know that. I can only beg you to give me the time I've requested. If you can't, then you'll do what you have to do.' Somehow giving in to him at this point seemed like good strategy, like rolling over and playing dead, going powerless before the enemy.

'Corbet, do you have any idea how exasperating you are?' Jouvet ran his tongue over his jagged teeth. 'You try my patience as no man ever has.'

'Yes, I can see that, Commissioner.' Corbet waited.

'Renard is continuing to find more evidence against Monique de La Tour. Obviously, I'm not going to tell you what it is. Suffice it to say that if you don't come up with an arrest that will stick within a day, she's our murderer. Is that perfectly understood?' Corbet had never had anyone glare at him with such animal ferocity.

'Yes, Commissioner, that's understood.' Corbet drew a deep breath and quietly sighed his relief. He had bought more time. He only hoped it would be enough.

Chapter Thirty-Four

The Café de Cluny had its usual late morning crowd. Corbet picked up the menu and stared at it somewhat blankly. His eye focused on the egg plate, a special with three fried eggs and juice. He suddenly had a craving. He would have it.

As the waiter left with his order, Corbet looked up to see Blanche Ballard rushing towards him, with her fur coat open and her hair flying everywhere.

'Inspector, I hope you realise how inconvenient these little meetings are for me. I do have a life to live, you know.' She sat down across from Corbet and began to tap the table with her long red nails.

'Yes, Madame Ballard, I'm sorry to trouble you, but there are a few more questions I must ask you in order to proceed with my investigation.' Corbet took a long sip of the coffee the waiter brought him. Blanche ordered a black coffee and began to pull out a cigarette from her purse. Corbet braced himself.

'Well, Inspector, this whole thing has upset my work life, to say nothing of my personal life. Georges hasn't been himself since this happened.' She gazed at Corbet with a cold, accusatory stare.

'Yes, I've noticed that Mr Lefèvre is not coping too well with the situation.' Corbet saw the distraught Lefèvre he had left half drunk in his office. He would need to talk to him again, too.

'To say the least, Inspector. He refuses to come home and has been living at his office for the past two days. He won't talk to me. What is it that you want of me now?' She blew her smoke right in Corbet's face.

'I'd like to know more about this.' Corbet batted the smoke away and handed her a Xerox copy of a review by Véronique Lefèvre of a book called *Autumn Song* by Blanche Ballard.

'Where did you dig this up, Inspector?' She blew another puff of smoke his way.

'I went to the library at the Centre Pompidou where they have all the back issues of the paper.' Corbet's eggs had arrived, and he began attacking the yellow yolks with pieces of broken bread.

'She wouldn't have said anything good about anything I did, and I think you know that, Inspector.' She challenged him with her eyes.

'But how did having her call your work a cheap imitation of Colette affect you, Madame Ballard? That's what concerns me.' Corbet swirled the yolks around on his plate.

'She really didn't know what she was talking about, and anyone who knew literature would know that. Just because I wrote a book about a relationship between a mature woman and a young man doesn't mean that I was imitating Colette. The tone and tenor of the relationships were entirely different.' She resumed tapping the table with her nails.

'But in both cases it appears that the young man finished rather badly?'

'What do you mean, Inspector? The young man in my book doesn't destroy himself.'

'But, Raymond appears to have met a bad end.' Corbet waited.

'Yes, Inspector, but that had nothing to do with his relationship with me.' She crushed out her cigarette.

'Didn't it?' Corbet waited while she lit yet another cigarette.

'Well, if you mean that Véronique Lefèvre might have killed her son to get him away from me, yes, I suppose you could say that. But I never had anything directly at all to do with his death.' Her long fingers trembled a little as she put the cigarette to her mouth.

'We don't know who had anything to do with his death, unfortunately.' Corbet drained his coffee cup.

'There's no way you could exhume the body and search for evidence of poison, Inspector?' She seemed relieved to have the attention focused elsewhere.

'Not unless he was poisoned with something other than the digitoxin that killed Véronique Lefèvre. I've looked into that. But now I'm afraid I must concentrate on the death of Véronique Lefèvre. We know that was murder.' He looked directly into Blanche's cold, little eyes. She finished her coffee and gathered her coat to leave.

'Inspector, I hope you'll forgive me, but I have to get to a meeting with my publisher. I don't want to be late.' She reached for her bill. Corbet took it out of her hand and motioned for her to exit the café.

'I'll get back to you later.' As he watched her go out the front door, something in the way she moved gave him a sense of déjà vu. Another piece of the puzzle fell into place.

Chapter Thirty-Five

The rain had begun to fall in earnest as Corbet trudged down the rue du Bac towards Georges Lefèvre's office. He had not called ahead. Surprise was always the best approach at times like this.

'I'm sorry, Inspector, but he hasn't come out of his office for at least twenty-four hours. Frankly, I'm quite concerned about him.' Martin looked as though he hadn't slept in some time. 'I'll let you in if you insist.' He headed for the door of Lefèvre's office.

'I've come to speak to you again, Monsieur Lefèvre,' Corbet said as he passed through the door into the darkened room full of stale air, cigarette smoke and the strong smell of Cognac. Georges Lefèvre was seated at his desk with his head leaning on his outstretched and folded arms. He was asleep. Corbet went over and gently shook his shoulders.

'What? What is it?' Lefèvre looked up into Corbet's eyes from a face that was drawn, lightly bearded and wrinkled with sleep.

'I just want a few words with you.' Corbet went to the large window and tried to open it up. Failing that, he opened the curtains to let some light in.

'Do you have to do that, Inspector?' Lefèvre covered his face with his hands.

'At least I need some light if I can't have fresh air. Why have you locked yourself up like this?' Corbet took the seat across from Lefèvre.

'It's all become too much for me, Inspector. It really has.' Lefèvre's demeanour was almost confessional.

'Yes, I imagine it has. Why did you lie to me about being away for a couple of days and about having nothing to do with that leak in the newspapers about Monique de La Tour's hair found at the scene?' The direct route would be best.

'Lie? Why, Inspector, I – yes, I was out of town, but not actually for as long as I told you. It's all very complicated. I was out of town on Tuesday afternoon on family business. That's all I'm going to say about it now.' Lefèvre's jaw seemed to harden with these words. Corbet couldn't risk letting his attitude set.

'Family business. Well, what kind of business was it that caused you to authorise the release of that information about the hair?'

'Inspector, it probably comes as no surprise to you that I have connections in some rather dark and murky places in the City of Paris.' Lefèvre reached for the almost empty bottle of Cognac and poured the rest of it into a dirty glass on his desk.

'Yes, but what does that have to do with reporting on evidence that hasn't been confirmed in a murder case?' Corbet got up and walked around his chair.

'A lot if you're getting pressure from all sides, Inspector. A lot, I assure you.' Lefèvre got up and went to the cabinet to look for more Cognac.

'Just who was it that was putting all of this pressure on you, Monsieur Lefèvre?' Corbet knew there was no hope of breathing clean air in the place.

'Your colleague, Inspector Renard, for one.' Lefèvre slunk back to his seat with a full Cognac bottle in his hand, sat down and poured himself a glass.

'Renard. I'm not surprised. I suspected something of the kind.'

'Yes, he came to me with the information and insisted that we print it or he would get one of our underground informers, Michel, at the Maison de Balzac to release some very incriminating evidence. He didn't say who it would incriminate. But I felt trapped. I couldn't take the chance that this would become a media trial of me for the murder of Véronique. I did what he asked me to do. There you have it, Inspector.' Lefèvre took a long drink of his comfort. But Corbet felt that he didn't have it at all, that he had only the tip of a rather unsightly iceberg.

'What do you know about this Michel? I know that every time I go to the Maison de Balzac I'm greeted with fumes of alcohol. What else does he do besides drink and implicate people in murder cases?' Corbet resumed his seat and shifted around to get as comfortable as possible.

'Well, if you must know, he's the head of a ring of petty thieves who do a lot of business on the streets of Paris. It's quite a network. They also often provide me with information, not always reliable, I might add, that I would never be able to get elsewhere. You could say he's one of my sources. I know that he has some pretty strong political connections which is why he hasn't lost his job in spite of his drunken behaviour. He's connected with some people over at the Préfecture, I'm sure. You mean to tell me you don't know about that, Inspector?' Lefèvre was going on the attack.

'No, as a matter of fact, I don't know about him specifically. I can assure you that I don't use the likes of him to get information about anything.' Corbet was beginning to get very angry and agitated. He had always known that Renard was a snake, but somehow the objective confirmation of this knowledge was disturbing.

'Yes, Inspector, Renard used Michel to put considerable pressure on me to print the information about the hair.' Lefèvre looked even more weary than he had when Corbet had first begun to speak to him.

'Well, I'm not surprised that he was behind it. He's doing everything possible to sabotage my efforts in this case.'

'Apparently so, Inspector.' Lefèvre drained his glass again.

'I don't want you to leave this place. I'm going to keep my men out front to see that you don't go anywhere. I'm only forewarning you.' Corbet rose and headed for the door.

'I don't think I'll be going anywhere, Inspector.' Lefèvre put his head back down on his folded arms.

On his way out, Corbet stopped at Martin's desk and asked to see Lefèvre's engagement diary for the past week. With some reluctance, Martin gave it up. Corbet poured over the pages and found the past Tuesday afternoon. Over the whole blank was written in large letters *LYON*.

Chapter Thirty-Six

Corbet wrapped his raincoat tighter around his large frame, put his head down under his umbrella and rushed over the Pont St Michel to the Préfecture. Gilet would be waiting for him.

Once inside his office, he took off his sopping coat and shook himself dry. Gilet came bursting into the office without knocking. Corbet stood for a moment and looked at him in silence.

'Sorry, Inspector, but I have so much to tell you.'

'Yes, I can see that.' Corbet went behind his desk and sat down.

'Those art dealers tell me that they've done business with Margot Dutemps for a number of years and that she has a daughter in Paris. They didn't know much more than that. They couldn't give me a name, an address or anything else. Just said that over the years she had mentioned a daughter.' Gilet clasped his long arms behind his back and waited.

'A daughter, you say. Very interesting. I knew she was lying to me.' Corbet sighed and reached into his drawer for a chocolate.

'I wish I had been able to get more for you, Inspector.' Gilet's soft eyes showed sympathy for the strain Corbet was obviously under.

'Nothing is what it seems, and no one means what he says. It's become a nightmare. All roads are beginning to lead to Lyon. I found out that Lefèvre had visited Lyon early last week when he was supposedly away for the dropping of the hair bomb.' Corbet got up and headed for his refrigerator. He opened a bottle of mineral water. He was beginning to feel in the grip of a constant indigestion from all of the frustration.

'Yes, Leroux is getting the final results on that other hair we found at the scene. I'm waiting for him to turn up now.' Gilet was trying to offer some comfort.

'Well, hurry up with it. I've got to talk to Jouvet and yet again beg him for more time and for immunity for Jacques. I'd like to have enough evidence to warrant getting it.'

There was a loud knock on the door and Corbet invited Leroux into the office.

'Inspector, we've matched the hair we found at the scene with a suspect.' Leroux put the report down in front of Corbet who took it in his hands and read it.

'Just as I was beginning to suspect. I've got to get to Jouvet right away.' He took the report and headed for the door.

Chapter Thirty-Seven

An early evening dark and hush had descended on the rue du Cardinal Lemoine. Corbet picked up his pace as he searched for Number 47. He found that it was a rather tired looking building next to a now-closed stationery store.

He rang the buzzer and was asked to identify himself. He did and was buzzed in. He didn't know why, but he felt somewhat surprised at that especially in light of his mission.

He took the small elevator up to the fourth floor and knocked on the door of Number 7. Blanche Ballard opened the door and without saying a word motioned for him to enter. Something in her posture and movement suggested a kind of resignation.

Corbet took the seat she offered him in the crowded, unkempt living room. As he sat down, he noticed a group of statues covered in dust on a table nearby. They were all elongated figures mostly of women's heads. With the low level of light in the room there was no way he could possibly identify the subjects.

'You know why I'm here, Madame Ballard?' Corbet waited.

'Yes, Inspector, I think I do. I've been waiting for you. I'm tired of the charade, almost glad the show is over.' She sank down into a worn leather chair opposite Corbet. Her hair was flying everywhere like that of her mother in Lyon.

'My men are outside waiting to help me take you in. You know you're under arrest for the murder of Véronique Lefèvre?'

'Yes, Inspector, I know that. My mother told me that you had visited her and had been inquiring about the bottle of digitoxin. I knew it wouldn't be long. She did her best to keep you away from me. I needn't tell you that I know I must have wanted to be caught or I would never have left that bottle where it could be found.' Her eyes seemed to have lost their cold fury.

'Yes, I gathered that, but it wasn't until we matched your hair with one found at the scene, and I spoke with Jacques who told me that Michel had let you in and out of the Maison de Balzac later that evening after you supposedly had left by the rear door that I knew for sure.' Corbet shifted in his seat.

'Yes, Inspector, it's never a good idea to trust those marginal types. They always have an angle and are ready at a moment's notice to sell you out.' She lit a cigarette and blew the smoke away from Corbet.

'Unlike Georges Lefèvre who seems to have tried to protect you in every way possible, even to the point of getting himself into trouble for withholding evidence.'

'Yes, poor Georges. He has taken this whole business rather hard, I'm afraid. But even he had begun to withdraw from me, though I know he never would have turned me in.' She stared off into space.

'But why would you work so hard to implicate Monique de La Tour? Was it only to throw the suspicion away from you?' Corbet got up and began to walk around the crowed, dusty room.

'In part, I suppose. You must know that I never cared much for her. I guess I felt that she had had undue influence over Raymond and was trying to interfere in our relationship by trying to urge a kind of celibacy on him. It had taken root and was a source of difficulty for us, I won't deny. I also felt that she had carried a torch for Georges for years. She was always lurking in the background, poised to make a move.' She smiled exposing her red gums.

'But there must have been more to it than that?' Corbet sat down again.

'Well, you know, Inspector, I'm pretty certain that Véronique Lefèvre murdered Raymond. He was the real love of my life, and those two women couldn't let me have him. Then when I became involved with Georges, Véronique was determined to try to stand in my way. I'll also admit that the bad review of my book didn't help much, either, although I doubt I would have killed her just for that even if I felt like it at the time.' She crushed out her cigarette.

'I see. But why did you use digitoxin? Why not some other type of poison?'

'At first it was only something handy, something available. I had been visiting with my mother, and I simply took her medication back to Paris with me. Then I realised the symbolic message of killing somebody at the Maison de Balzac during an award dinner by using coffee and digitoxin. You must know, Inspector, that Balzac was a coffee addict and that that no doubt contributed to his productivity as well as his death?' She lit another cigarette.

'Yes, I know that. You couldn't resist the literary touch?' Corbet frowned and shifted in his seat. This woman was unappealing even in her confessional state.

'No, and I only helped Véronique do what she was determined to do anyway, kill herself with drugs. The autopsy must have shown that?' She blew smoke directly at Corbet who leaned to one side to avoid it.

'It did.' Corbet was beginning to feel very weary and merely wanted to take her into the Préfecture.

'What will happen with Georges? I hope he'll be all right.' Her eyes softened.

'We'll have to arrest him for withholding information at least.' Corbet sighed as the broken image of Lefèvre came to view.

'Do be gentle with him. I think he's at the end of his rope, Inspector.' Blanche got up and went over to the window and looked out.

'We'll do only what we have to do, Madame Ballard. You'll have to come with me. I'll speak with you further down at the Préfecture.' Blanche Ballard rose from her seat, and Inspector Corbet led her out the door and down the stairs to join his men in the street.

Chapter Thirty-Eight

'How fitting it is, Henri, that we should celebrate your promotion to Chief Inspector at Au Pied de Voltaire, the oldest coffee house in Paris once frequented by Balzac, Hugo, Voltaire, and Rousseau.' Marie beamed at Chief Inspector Corbet as they ascended the large staircase leading to the private room at the top which the restaurant had set up for the fête.

They entered the room and proceeded to a long table at the back where Gilet, Leroux, Ménager, Henriette, and Monique De La Tour were seated.

'Hail to the Chief!' They all stood up and lifted their glasses of champagne in a toast to Chief Inspector Henri Corbet.

'It has been a long and difficult journey, and I thank you all.' Corbet was deeply touched. He grabbed Marie's hand and led her to the head of the table where two places had been reserved.

'Renard won't bother you any more, Inspector. I know for a fact that Jouvet let him go today.' Gilet's enthusiasm was comforting. 'Not only will he not get the promotion to Chief Inspector, he'll never work in law enforcement again when they're through with him.'

'Yes, he was charged with trying to corrupt an ongoing investigation. He won't come back from those kind of allegations.' Leroux rubbed his hands together and smiled at Corbet.

Chief Inspector Corbet cleared his throat and looked at his admiring audience. 'In a case filled with twists and turns and all kinds of strange relationships, I think the most surprising discovery was that Renard had been Véronique Lefèvre's old lover. The handwriting on the love letters I found in her apartment matched his. It explains why he was so very eager to make an arrest in the case. He knew that if he were ever connected with Véronique Lefèvre, he would never get the promotion to Chief Inspector. He thought he could keep a lid on the sewer by convicting Monique of the murder of her sister.' Chief Inspector Corbet signed and smiled gently.

'You men know that I couldn't have done any of it without you. And certainly not without you, Jean-Pierre.' Corbet nodded his head towards Ménager who held his glass up once again in a toast.

'To the new Chief Inspector, my warmest congratulations and my pledge of ongoing service.' His blue eyes twinkled.

'Thank you, Jean-Pierre.'

'Inspector, I must tender you my most heart-felt thanks for clearing my name and taking the tarnish from my triumph.' Monique de La Tour lifted her glass to Corbet.

'My pleasure. No matter how bad the evidence looked, my instincts told me that you weren't capable of murder.' Corbet lifted his glass back to the beautiful and more relaxed Monique de La Tour.

'I'm very grateful to you, Henri – I mean, Chief Inspector Corbet, for helping during this most difficult time.' Henriette lowered her eyes and then looked back up at Corbet.

'Henriette, without your courage and willingness to disclose what you knew, I would still be a long way from solving the case. I'm very indebted to you and not at all unmindful of the sacrifices you've made.' Corbet lifted his glass to Henriette and the whole table followed suit.

'To Henriette!' they all exclaimed.

'Thank you all. Thank you.' Henriette blushed and raised her glass back to the assembly. While Jacques had been granted immunity from prosecution because of the information he had provided about Michel's activities, he was nonetheless required to leave the Maison de Balzac, and, certainly, his relationship with Henriette was over.

'You have more strength than you realise, Henriette.' Corbet smiled gently at her. He knew that she would make it through this difficult time and that in the long run she would be better off without the cad who had been her life companion.

'Again, I thank you all.' Corbet stood and lifted his glass.

'Oh, Henri, look.' The waiters were bringing in large silver platters of salmon with champagne sauce, the main course for the evening's celebration.

'Yes, Marie, we're going to eat well once again.' Corbet took her hand in his and squeezed it lightly.

Epilogue

As the TGV sped down the tracks towards Nice, Corbet shifted in his seat, looked over at Marie and his heart leapt for joy. They were going to stay at the elegant Negresco. Chief Inspector Corbet looked forward to reconnecting with his Provençal roots and to beginning a new phase of his relationship with Marie. Promise and light were everywhere.